BETTER
THAN A
BROTHER

To

Missouri Center for the Book—

Edith McCall

Sept. 13, 1993

BETTER THAN A BROTHER

by
Edith McCall

Walker & Company
New York

Library of Congress Cataloging-in-Publication Data

McCall, Edith S.
Better than a brother / by Edith McCall.
p. cm.—(Walker's American history series for young people)
Summary: The adventures of a young girl growing up at the turn of the century on the shores of Lake Monona in Madison, Wisconsin, where her family ran a boarding house for ice cutters.
ISBN 0-8027-6782-6. ISBN 0-8027-6783-4 (lib. bdg.).
[1. Family life—Fiction. 2. Wisconsin—Fiction.] I. Title.
II. Series.
PZ7.M1229Be 1988   87-27369
[Fic]—dc19   CIP
AC

Printed in the United States of America

10 9 8 7 6 5 4 3 2 1

Text design by Laurie McBarnette

The James May family, from left to right:
Beth, Mother, Martin, Mary (Hughie), James,
Nora, Dad

A NOTE FROM THE AUTHOR

Years ago, when we were on a trip to Madison, Wisconsin, my mother pointed out to me a row of willow trees growing along the north shore of Lake Monona, in Madison, Wisconsin. She told me that for a while when she was a girl, her family lived in a big house just back of those trees, and that the trees had been planted as twigs by her mother.

Mother told me more about her mother—the grandmother I never knew. In 1886, Ellen Hughes married James May, who had come to America from Ireland. In the 1890's, when my mother, their first child, was about nine years old, they moved into a huge white house on the shore of Lake Monona, a boarding house for ice cutters, owned by the Knickerbocker Ice Company. Each winter, my grandmother cooked for a crew of men who worked for the ice company when they came to cut ice.

"Your grandmother could do anything, from sewing the clothes for all six of us children to helping us build an iceboat," Mother told me. She remembered the butter her mother made for sale and refrigerated in the huge building, next to their home, where ice was stored. She told about the St. Bernard dog they had—

and a cruel workman who pushed the dog into the open water where the men had cut the ice away.

From my mother's memories this story grew in my imagination. The James May family became the James Riley family, and Mary May became my Ellen Hughes Riley, "Hughie" in the story. I learned more about the business of cutting and storing ice and of life in 1900, before the electric refrigerator was invented, and it all became very real to me.

I hope you enjoy reading *Better Than a Brother* as much as I enjoyed writing it!

Your friend,
Edith McCall

*For my mother,
the oldest child
in an icehouse family*

CHAPTER * 1

"Hugh-ie! Help me! It was a sad wail. "Help me, ple-ease, Hughie."

That late December day in 1899, Hughie Riley heard her little sister, Beth, but she just went on packing wet snow into balls. She was crouched behind a snow-fort wall that faced another snow fort about fifty feet away. Faithfully, Barney, the big St. Bernard dog, sat beside her, watching the ammunition pile grow.

"Hugh-ie-ee—" Little Beth's wail came again. Hughie looked down at her red-mittened hands and went on shaping the snowball. Barney touched Hughie's shoe with a big paw and looked at her, his eyes more sorrowful than usual.

"Okay, Barney," Hughie said, and raised her voice. "What's the matter, Beth?"

"M-my rubber—came off—and I c-c-can't get it back on!"

"Oh, drat. Double drat," Hughie muttered. "Barney, I wish you could go over there and put it on for her.

Barney looked at her and sighed.

"Just a minute, Bethie!" Hughie called out. She packed another good solid snowball, placed it on top of the pyramid of ammunition, and started to leave the fort. A snowball hit her shoulder. She ducked back behind the wall.

"Bethie, tell Nora to put it back on for you!" she yelled. "Hey, you guys! No fair!"

"All's fair in love and war, Hughie!" Jim yelled back. "Come on, let's get this battle going!"

"Scaredy-cat! Stand up and fight!" Marty's voice.

Hughie peeked over her wall and then dropped down again. The boys were nowhere in sight. "Stand up yourselves! You're the scaredy-cats!"

She packed another snowball and turned to her left. She could see the back porch of their big white frame house. Beth, four years old, sat on the top step, only her eyes and nose visible between the blue tam pulled down over her forehead and the matching scarf over her chin. Two steps down from Beth, eight-year-old Nora, equally bundled up, was trying to force the rubber over the heel of Beth's shoe.

Hughie returned to making more snowballs. Cautiously peering over her wall, she couldn't see the boys, but a well-aimed snowball caught her before she dropped down again.

"Barney, it's not fair," she said. "The boys stick together. I sure wish Nora was bigger and not such a sissy. But she can't even throw straight. If you could, you'd fight on my side, wouldn't you? But I have to lick 'em all by myself."

Barney gave an understanding grunt.

The enemy crouched safely behind the other snow wall, reinforced the evening before by water carefully poured over it. Jim, ten and a half, and Marty, nine, had challenged Hughie to a snowball battle, insisting that their big sister's advanced age of thirteen—almost grown up, they maintained—made two against one a fair fight.

"And you can have Barney," Jim had conceded.

Cautiously, snowball in hand, Hughie looked through a peephole. Neither boy was in sight. Beyond their lumpy snow wall she could see Lake Monona, frozen and snow-covered, white except where strong winds had swept the snow away from the gray-blue ice.

She packed her snowball a bit more, about to open battle, when the wail came again.

"Hughie! Nora can't get it on!"

Nora added her soprano. "Hughie! Come and help!"

Hughie sighed and put down her ammunition. "Barney, sometimes I wish I was the baby of this family, 'stead of the oldest!" she grumbled. Then she called loudly in the direction of the enemy fort. "Hey, fellas! I gotta go on a mission of mercy. I declare a truce while I help Bethie."

Two stocking-capped heads came partly into view above the enemy wall.

"No fair firing until I can get back in my fort!" she yelled. "Do you hear me? Promise not to attack while I'm out in the open!"

The two boys whispered together. Then Jim shouted, "Okay, Hughie. We promise not to fire while you're helping Beth. But make it fast!"

Hughie left her fort, Barney at her heels. "Don't you dare break your promise!" she called out to the enemy.

Brushing snow from her long, heavy coat, she strode toward the back porch, past the snow family Nora and Beth had been making. Nora had given up on Beth's rubber and was rolling a large snowball to form the midsection of the biggest snow person, obviously the father. At the top of the four gray steps, Beth stood on one foot, holding the porch post with one hand and a shiny black rubber with the other.

As Hughie reached the porch, Beth's face puckered. "Hurry, Hughie," she said. "My leg is tired of holding me up so long."

Hughie sighed. "All right, all right, hold your horses! Here, give me that rubber and sit down." She swept a spot clear of snow and helped her little sister keep her coat under her as she sat on the top step.

Pulling off her mittens, Hughie tried to get the rubber over Beth's shoe. "Why did this come off, Bethie? It fits so tight!"

"I was just trying to scrape off a chunk of snow so's I wouldn't slip," Beth said. Then she cried out, "Hughie, don't push so hard! You're hurting me!"

"There it goes. Now see that it stays on." Hughie straightened up and pulled her red stocking cap down to meet her scarf. She remembered, guiltily, the new gold locket and chain she was wearing, against her mother's advice, and felt to make sure it was still in place. Satisfied, she rewrapped her scarf, put her mittens back on, and glanced over at her brother's fort.

"Keep an eye on them, Barney," she said, and turned back to smile at Beth. "Come on, baby. I'll help you down the steps." She took the little girl's hand and gave her a quick hug as she released her. "Now you can go back to your snow people."

Nora was struggling to lift the oversized snowball body into place.

"Let me help you hoist that, Nora," Hughie said and the snowman grew two feet taller.

"Thanks, Hughie," Nora said. "Now I'll make his head."

"Okay, you two, don't get in any more trouble. I've got a fight to win."

She bent over to scoop up some snow. As she rose, a well-packed missile struck her shoulder. Another hit her waist. The two boys stood in plain sight behind their fort, looking pleased with themselves and ready to fire again.

"No fair! You promised!" Hughie yelled. "Wait'll I get you!"

Jim sent another well-aimed snowball at his sister. "Only promised to hold off while you helped Beth!" he shouted.

Holding a big clump of snow, Hughie ran toward the two boys. Barney barked joyously at her side. "You're going to get your smarty face washed real clean, Jim Riley!" she yelled.

Both boys ran toward the frozen lake. A hugh ice-house blocked the way to the right. They crossed the spur railroad track that ran between the icehouse and the lake. Hughie ran faster. Beyond the tracks, she passed Marty. On she ran, after Jim, down the gentle slope that edged the lake and out onto the ice.

Jim's taunting voice came back to her. "Hughie, Hughie, can't catch me; Hughie-dewey, can't catch a fly!"

Hughie wasted no breath on words. After Jim she went, gaining on him with every step. But Jim had a good head start. He slipped a time or two but kept going farther out onto the snow-covered ice.

Off to the west, beyond the end of the icehouse, some boys were playing ice hockey. One of them turned and waved as the boys and Hughie went out into the open.

Jim yelled, "There's your boyfriend, Hughie! Jerry's waving at you'!"

Hughie turned to look and lost her footing. Down she went, sliding along on her back. The wind had blown the ice almost clean of snow, but a thin, powdery covering was left that made it extra slippery.

All she could think of was how she must look. She scrambled to her feet as best she could and was relieved to see that the neighbor boys had turned their full attention to their hockey puck. As she got up, Jim stopped a few feet away.

"Can't catch me! Call your sweetheart to come and help, Hughie-dewey!" he taunted. As his sister reached for him, he dodged to one side. Suddenly his feet went out from under him and he slid along on the seat of his knickers. His feet, looking huge in their one-buckle overshoes, were high in the air.

"Gotcha!" yelled Hughie. She threw herself down on Jim, pushing snow into his face.

Barney barked and pranced about. Marty stood back, cheering Jim on.

"How'd you like that, smarty!" Hughie straightened up a bit to enjoy the sight of Jim's Santa Claus snow beard. But her victory was brief. The boy grabbed her scarf and pulled her back down, and they rolled over and over on the ice. Finally, Jim let go of Hughie's scarf to protect himself, and Hughie got a chance to pin his arms down and kneel on him.

"Say uncle!" she demanded. Jim struggled.

"*Say uncle!*" Hughie repeated, pushing Jim down with each word.

"Okay, okay—uncle."

He started to get up and Hughie pushed him down again. Barney started to lick the snow from his face, but Jim pushed the dog away with his mittened hands.

"No fair. You've got Barney helping you."

Hughie pretended not to hear. "You didn't keep your promise."

"Did too. Never promised not to get you on the way back."

Just then a call came from the back porch of the Riley house, a call they knew better than to ignore.

"Hughie, Jim, Marty—all of you! Get in here right away!"

It was Mama calling. "Coming, Mama!" Hughie called. Mama didn't like it when she didn't get an answer. Reluctantly, Hughie let Jim get up.

"Be quick about it," they heard Mama say as she closed the back door.

Jim, on his feet again, scooped up some snow and grabbed the end of Hughie's scarf. She pulled away, leaving the scarf in Jim's hand and ran as fast as she could without slipping, trying to keep from falling over Barney. All three children were laughing by now. Hughie darted ahead.

"Wait for me, Hughie," she heard Jim say. "Don't you want your scarf?"

But she kept on toward the house, pulling off her

mittens. As she reached the back porch, she thought again of her beautiful locket. Grandma had given it to her for Christmas two days ago, and Mama had told her not to wear it except for special occasions, but she loved it so much she had put it on anyway.

She was feeling for it under her coat collar when Jim came stealthily up behind her. He said, "Here's your scarf, Hughie. And something else for your neck."

She hardly felt the chill of snow down her neck and made no attempt to grab hold of Jim. Frantically, she felt for the chain and locket, snatched her scarf, and checked it too. They were gone! She'd better get back out on the lake to find them—

Mama, a shawl around her shoulders, came back onto the porch. Picking up the broom to sweep snow from the little girls' coats and rubbers, she saw Hughie heading back toward the lake.

"Hughie, where are you going? Get in here right away. Your grandma is leaving!"

Hughie's heart sank as she climbed the steps to the porch.

Mama and the two smaller girls were going inside. "Hurry now," she said, handing the broom to Hughie, who was almost gentle as she swept snow from Marty's coat.

"What's the matter, Hughie?" Jim asked. "Want me to sweep the snow off your coat?"

"Yes, please," Hughie said.

Jim and Marty looked at each other puzzled. "She must be sick," Marty said. "Wake her up with the broom, Jim."

But Jim saw the troubled look on Hughie's face. "Truce, Marty," he said.

CHAPTER *2

The cold storeroom smelled of wet wool. Mama had just spread the girls' scarves, hats, and mittens on the drying rack. As Hughie came in, the boys were taking off their overshoes.

Mama, with Beth and Nora in tow, was about to open the door that led into the kitchen. She looked back and said, "Hughie, hurry. Grandma has to leave for the depot in a very few minutes." The railroad depot was in the middle of Madison, Wisconsin. The Rileys lived in Blooming Grove, just east of the city.

"She's leaving today? I thought she was staying over New Year's." Hughie was unbuckling her new three-buckle overshoes, another of her Christmas presents. The Riley family was planning a special New Year's celebration Sunday evening because midnight would bring a new century as well as a new year.

"I'll tell you all why she's leaving when you're inside. But please hurry." And with that Mama closed the door behind her.

"Gee," Jim said. "I thought Grandma would be here when 1899 ends and 1900 begins. She won't see any more new centuries start."

"You won't either, Jim, unless you live to be an old man of a hundred and ten!" Hughie said.

She was taking off her heavy, greenish-black coat. It

was a bit too large but made new for her this winter from her father's old overcoat, with the unworn inside of his old coat now the outside of Hughie's new one.

A row of pegs was on the wall across from the drying rack, each marked with a family member's name. Hughie hung the coat on her peg. "Golly, I love having Grandma here, even if I do have to share my room with her. I wonder why she's leaving so soon." She added her red stocking cap, scarf, and mittens to the collection on the drying rack.

The warm air from the kitchen came into the back room as Mama opened the door again. "Come on, you three," she said. "Grandma has to catch the five fifty-five train back to Chicago. A telegram came about an hour ago. Grandma is needed at home because Aunt Effie is sick."

Hey, that's too bad," Marty said. He and Jim followed Mama into the kitchen.

Hughie took a moment more to check her coat to see if the locket had caught in the lining. "Shucks," she muttered when the search proved fruitless. "I'll have to go back on the lake as soon as Grandma's gone and find it."

In the kitchen, the warmth from the big old iron cookstove felt good, but Hughie couldn't linger. As she passed the table, she did bend over for one delicious whiff of the loaves of freshly baked bread set there to cool. Then she went into the huge, chilly dining room, seldom used except when the ice company crew was here, toward the front parlor.

"Isn't Ellen coming to say goodbye? The hackman will be here any minute."

It was Grandma's voice. Grandma was the only one who called Hughie "Ellen," although that was her real name. She and Mama and Grandma all had the same names, Ellen Hughes Riley—except that Grandma wasn't a Riley. "Hughie" was better than having to be "little Ellen" or "big Ellen," the family agreed—all except Grandma, who thought Hughie sounded like a boy's name and refused to use it.

The Riley family was gathered in the parlor—which was really the ice company boss's office—except for baby Rose—and Papa, of course. He was working at the railroad yards in Madison.

Grandma, ready to go, stood near the Christmas tree. She looked beautiful, Hughie thought, in her long navy-blue velvet coat, with her white hair showing a little under the big hat that matched the coat. She was really elegant, and she smelled wonderful too. Hughie loved Grandma's lavender cologne. She'd even used a drop or two herself while the bottle was on her bedroom dresser, along with Grandma's silver-backed brush and comb and mirror.

Grandma reached out to hug her eldest grandchild. "Oh, Grandma," Hughie said, "I wish you didn't have to leave so soon. We'll miss you! Tell Aunt Effie to get better fast."

"Stop talking a minute and listen," Grandma said. "I want to whisper something in your ear."

Hughie saw a twinkle in her grandmother's blue eyes as she turned her head to hear the secret.

"I've left my cologne bottle on your dresser with a little still in it," Grandma whispered. "Use it when you dress up and wear your locket."

"I heard you, Grandma!" Jim said gleefully. "Hughie's gonna use that smelly toilet water!"

Hughie ignored her brother. "Grandma, I love you. Come back as soon as you can. And thanks so much for the locket. It's so pretty." Suddenly, Hughie felt her face growing red.

Grandma leaned over to hug little Nora and Beth. Hughie's guilty blush had paled by the time Grandma straightened and spoke to her again.

"That locket is special for my namesake, Ellen," she said. "It's heart-shaped for sweethearts. Your grandfather gave it to me before we were married." Her voice seemed to choke up a bit. But when she went on, there was a twinkle in her eyes. "I took out the old pictures and put my favorite picture of you on the girl's side, honey. You can choose the picture for the other side later."

Marty had been standing at the window, holding back the lace curtain. "Here comes your sleigh, Grandma," he called out. "Hear the bells jingling?"

"Beautiful sound," Grandma said. "But that means it's time for me to go."

In another minute the front door was open. The hackman came in, bundled against the cold. "I'll take your bags out, Mrs. Hughes. Now watch your step."

"I'll help her," Jim said.

Grandma was hugging Mama. "Kiss the baby goodbye for me, Ellen. And don't work yourself to death taking care of that ice crew!" With Jim on her right side to keep her from slipping, she walked carefully out to the sleigh, holding up her coat to keep it from the snow and showing her beautiful gray kid high-button shoes.

As she climbed into the cutter, she called back, "I'll write as soon as I can! And Happy New Year to you all!"

"Happy New Year!" they all called.

"And Happy New Century too, Grandma!" Hughie added.

The driver tucked a lap robe around his passenger and picked up the reins. The horse took off on the snowy road with a toss of his head and a jingle of the sleigh bells.

Then Grandma was gone, and the front door closed behind Jim as he came back inside. They were all quiet as they listened to the sleigh bells' music fading in the distance.

Jim shivered. "Br-r-r-r. I feel like I was in the ice-house. It's getting colder, Mama."

"And that reminds me," Mama said. "Two telegrams came—not just the one for your grandma. The Knickerbocker Ice Company crew is arriving on January second. That's next Tuesday!"

"Oh, no." Jim groaned. "We were going to fix up the iceboat and have some fun before they cut away all the good ice."

"If we all pitch in, maybe you'll have most of New Year's Day to be out there," Mrs. Riley said. "But we've got to clean the whole house, and get twenty beds ready in the dormitory, and bake lots of bread and pies."

The house the Rileys lived in was owned by the ice company. In exchange for providing a place where the work crew could live during the month of ice cutting each winter, Mr. Riley didn't have to pay any rent. But

Mama had to have plenty of food ready for the hungry men three times a day.

"Mama, I hope that awful man won't be back this year," Hughie said.

"What man, dear?"

"You know. The one I told you about. I think they called him Cass."

"You mean the skinny guy with the droopy mustache?" Jim asked. "I didn't like him either. He was always bossing Mart and me around. Did he boss you, too, Hughie? Is that why you don't like him?"

"Never mind now, Jim. It's a secret between Hughie and me," Mama said. She put an arm around Hughie's shoulders, as they started toward the kitchen, and said in a low voice, "If he does come, dear, keep away from him as much as you can. And Hughie—let Papa and me know if he does anything like that again."

"Yes, Mama. But I hope he doesn't come."

They reached the kitchen, and Hughie's mind went back to her lost locket. Papa would be home soon, but if she hurried she could go back out and search for it before she had to help Mama get supper ready. She started toward the door to the storeroom.

Just then Rose piped up from the bedroom where she had been napping.

"Honey, please get the baby up for me," Mama called after Hughie. "And tell the boys to get out here and fill the woodboxes. I need to get the fire built up so I can start supper."

Hughie turned back reluctantly. "Yes, Mama." She passed on the message to Marty and Jim and then went into the big bedroom that Mr. and Mrs. Riley shared.

Rose's crib was against one wall. "Come on, baby. My goodness! You're still dry! Good girl." She busied herself getting eighteen-month-old Rose onto her potty chair.

"Hurry, baby, so's your big sister can go find her locket."

"Wocket?" Rose repeated.

"Sh-h-h, honey. Just hurry."

A few minutes later, Hughie had turned the baby over to Nora to be watched. Again she headed for the kitchen and the back door. Mama was filling a kettle with water from the bucket on the sink shelf.

"Where are you going, Hughie?"

Hughie paused, hand on the doorknob. "I've got to go down the path, Mama." The outhouse would be as good an excuse as any.

"Well, while you have your coat on, dear, go to the cellar and get some more potatoes and a jar of beans. Oh, and a jar of peaches, too. And hurry, Hughie. I don't have enough potatoes here for supper."

"Yes, Mama."

"Don't forget to take the basket with you."

"Yes, Mama. I mean, no, Mama. I won't forget. But I may not be able to get back real quick—"

"Quick as you can then, dear. Papa will be home soon."

Hughie hurried into her coat and overshoes. Taking the basket from its hook on the wall, she went out. She could hear the boys over beyond the woodpile. Barney bounded toward her joyfully.

"Can't play now, Barney," she said. She set the basket down near the outhouse door and went on toward the lake, Barney at her heels. They followed the trail in the snow that she and her brothers had made to the place on the ice where she had caught up with Jim. It was easy to see just where she'd had him down on his back.

"Oh, Barney," she said. "I wish you could find it for me." The dog snuffled about in the snow as if he knew what she meant.

Quickly Hughie scanned the ice, but there was no glint of gold. She brushed away some of the snow, her hands growing redder and colder every second. When she knew she'd taken as long as she dared, she slowly retraced her route over the ice, watching in vain for a bright bit of metal.

"Sure wish Mama wasn't waiting for me, Barney," she said. "Gotta go in now, but we'll come back out in the morning when I have more time to search."

She stopped briefly in the outhouse. When she came out, Barney had retired to his doghouse and the boys were going into the house with armloads of wood. Thoroughly chilled and heavy-hearted, Hughie picked up the basket and headed around the side of the house to the cellar entrance, a low, slanting wooden door that covered a few steps cut into the ground below.

She took hold of the metal handle on the door to lift it. "Ooh—that's cold!" She let go so quickly that the door dropped with a bang and she had to raise it again. Another door at the foot of the steps led to the cellar, where root vegetables and the home-canned products of last summer's garden were stored.

"I hate this place!" she said as she went down the steps and opened the door. She felt on a ledge to the right for a candle in its holder and put her hand into a spider web. "Ish! I double-hate this place!"

As quickly as her chilled fingers would allow, she opened the jar that held the wooden matches and struck one on the stone foundation wall. Her fingers were so cold she could scarcely hold the flame to the candle wick.

Hurriedly, she took the jars of beans and peaches from the wooden shelves that lined the cellar room and put them in the basket. She reached into a burlap sack to get potatoes. With the basket full, she put the candle back in its place and blew it out.

As she lowered the cellar door again, her teeth were chattering—a good accompaniment for the thoughts jumping about in her head. Where could her locket be? How was she ever going to find it with all that snow? And what would Mama say when she found out that Hughie had worn it when she wasn't supposed to?

CHAPTER *3

"Here's everything you told me to get, Mama."

Hughie tried to sound cheerful as she set the basket on the big oilcloth-covered table where her mother was peeling potatoes. Mama put one into a pan of water to wash as she finished paring off the last bit of skin.

"Thank you, Hughie. Finish peeling the potatoes while I put the pork chops on to cook. Marty! Jim!" she called out. Mrs. Riley had work for each of them—feeding the cow, Bessie (Mama was the only one Bessie would allow to milk her), getting water from the well, taking ashes from the heating stoves, and bringing in coal and more wood.

Jim and Marty returned to the kitchen for their assignments. Hughie was peeling potatoes when Jim purposely bumped against her as he walked toward the door. Hughie pretended not to notice.

"What's the matter with you, Hughie?" Jim asked when she didn't react. "You sick or somethin'?"

"I guess a person can act grown up once in a while," Hughie said distantly. Chin in the air, she gave a toss of her head that bounced her chestnut-brown braids back onto her shoulders.

"That's what Mama keeps telling you, Hughie, but I don't think you'll *ever* be a lady," Jim shot back as he left the kitchen.

Hughie could not think of anything to say. Her mind went back to the lost locket as she cut away the brown potato peel. She'd have to find a reason to stay out on the ice longer. The locket just had to be there, and she'd better find it before Mama discovered it was missing.

She got some more potatoes from the basket and took them to the sink to clean off the garden mud. At one end of the sink was a small pump that brought water from the cistern, a tank where rainwater from the roof was collected to use for washing. As she filled the tin basin in the sink, she tried to figure out how and where she had lost the locket.

Guess I didn't get the fastener on the gold chain closed just right, she thought. Or maybe the chain broke—it was awfully old.

Could it be out by the porch where she'd put on Bethie's rubber? No, she'd felt it still in place right afterward. Most likely it had come loose when she was chasing Jim or rolling around on the ice.

"I've just got to get out there," she said aloud.

Carrying Rose, Mrs. Riley returned to the kitchen as Hughie was speaking.

"What did you say, dear?" she asked.

Hughie was putting her parings—some of them too thick to stand Mama's inspection—into the garbage bucket that stood on the floor next to the sink. "Oh, nothing, Mama. Just thinking out loud, I guess." She quickly washed the potatoes again as Mrs. Riley lowered the baby into her high chair.

Hughie took the potatoes over to the huge black iron cookstove that kept the spacious kitchen so warm. It had lots of nickel trim on the doors, engraved with fancy designs. Polishing the trim was one of Hughie's weekly duties. On the stovetop were six cooking holes, each with an iron cover, and at one end there was a "reservoir." This was kept filled with cistern water so there would always be warm water for washing, and Papa could shave himself comfortably every Sunday morning. A teakettle with well water for cooking was heating at the back of the stove.

Hughie transferred the potatoes to a cooking pot and poured water from the teakettle over them. She set the pot into one of the cooking holes next to the firebox and refilled the teakettle with water from a blue-and-white enameled bucket at the sink.

"There, Mama. The potatoes are on to cook." It was still not quite dark outside; maybe she could go out again for a few minutes.

"Did you shake down the ashes?" Mama asked. "We need a good hot fire."

Hughie turned back to the stove, inserted the special handle into the front of the firebox, and moved it noisily from side to side.

Then she started toward the door to the storeroom, but Mama stopped her again. "Hughie, dear, will you get a cup of milk for the baby and help her with it while I turn the chops?"

It just wasn't fair. "Can't Nora do that?"

"Hughie! Please do as I ask. Nora and Beth are folding the clean clothes. I've got to go milk Bessie, you know that."

Hughie knew better than to say aloud what she was thinking: I hate being the oldest! I always gotta do everything! She'd have to wait until morning for another chance to look for the locket.

As she helped little Rose hold the cup of milk, Hughie made her plans. Papa got up before daylight, because he had to be at the railroad yards by seven o'clock. Mama was the first one in the kitchen, to cook breakfast for Papa while he washed and dressed. He had to be on his way before six thirty, and then Mama would go back to her bedroom to dress before she went out to milk Bessie.

All Hughie had to do was watch for the moments after Papa left and before Mama came out to the kitchen again. If she was very, very quiet and stayed away from the creaky floorboard, she could go outside without anyone's knowing she was even out of bed. That's what she would do. The hardest part would be making herself wake up early.

Papa was home. She could hear him stamping his feet on the back porch to get the snow off his shoes. Marty and Mama came in with him. A blast of cold air rushed into the kitchen before the storeroom door was closed again. Mr. Riley leaned over for Hughie to plant a kiss on his cold cheek.

"How's my big girl today?" he asked as he turned to kiss the baby on her forehead.

"All right, Papa."

Papa walked over to the sink to wash. "You don't sound quite like your usual perky self." Hughie was saved from having to answer, for Mama began telling him about Grandma's having to leave and the fact that the ice crew was coming in less than a week. Nora and

Beth set the table as Hughie put the beans on the stove to heat.

Jim was already seated at his usual place, and Marty was standing on a chair to light the kerosene lamp that hung from the ceiling above the table. He adjusted the wick, and light glowed cheerfully through the dome-shaped white glass shade.

"Slice some bread, Hughie, while I drain the potatoes," Mama said.

Five minutes later, all eight Rileys were seated at the oval table. Mama's place was at the end nearest the stove. To her left, away from the stove, was Rose's high chair. Hughie's place was on the baby's left, with Beth beside her, closest to Papa, who sat at the head of the table. Next came Jim. Nora sat between Jim and Marty, "to keep peace in the family as much as possible," Mama said.

Papa's curly, sandy-colored hair was still dark from his wet comb. The smell of tar soap came to the table with him. The children had been taught that they were not to start chattering as soon as they were seated, before Papa had finished the blessing. The food was passed to him first, eyed hungrily by the children as they saw it go by.

Papa was always given the chance to start the conversation, too, in the way he had learned as a boy in Ireland, when he had had to wait for his father to speak first. Papa had come to the United States twenty years ago, when he was twenty-nine. There was still much of old Ireland in the way he talked, in spite of the fact that he was proud to be an American citizen.

"America—'tis the land of opportunity," he often

said. Sometimes Hughie tried to say it as he did, with her tongue making the r's roll a bit, and that different sound Papa gave to the vowels of the words. But Papa didn't like her to imitate him. He wanted his children to be real Americans.

"You boys see that you study hard so you can get better jobs than mine. Then you'll have no problem feeding your own families," he said, as he helped himself to the boiled potatoes and gravy. "Have you done your homework today?"

"Papa! This is Christmas vacation!" Marty said.

Papa snorted. He could be very stern. But Hughie looked up from working the good gravy into her potatoes and saw that he had that twinkle she loved in his blue eyes. He was about to try to make them all laugh.

"Now then," he said when all the plates were loaded and most of the mouths full, "which one of you upset your grandma and made her leave so soon?" His voice was still stern as he questioned each of them.

When he got to Jim, he asked, very seriously, "Jim, did you pelt Grandma with snowballs?"

"No, sir. Only Hughie." Jim grinned.

"But he and Marty cheated!" Hughie put in.

"Silence, daughter!" Papa sounded fierce. "This is serious business."

Papa's stare made Hughie giggle and she ducked her head.

"Baby, did you put oatmeal in Granny's hair?"

Now they all laughed. "You're right that time, James," Mama said. "Rose did put oatmeal in Grandma's hair this morning. But Grandma wouldn't let a little thing like that drive her away."

Papa turned to Beth. "Beth, did you make faces at her?"

Beth giggled. She and Nora immediately made faces at each other across the table.

"Nora!" Papa's voice was so stern that Nora's newest grimace didn't quite disappear. "See there? I told you your face would freeze in one of those ugly looks. Now let's see my pretty girl again. . . . That's better. What did you do to scare away your poor grandma?"

Nora almost always took Papa seriously. She said in a small voice, "Nothing, Papa, honest! I used her powder puff once, but she said it was all right."

"Well, it must have been Hughie. Hughie, did you push your poor old grandmother out of bed?"

Hughie had let her mind drift away from the family banter. She was thinking about how Grandma had given her that locket because she was so grown up, and now she'd lost it because she had acted anything *but* grown up. "Ladylike" was Mama's way of saying it— and she was anything but ladylike, roughhousing with the boys.

Suddenly she became aware that the whole family was looking at her.

"Aha! Guilt is written all over your face, Ellen Hughes Riley!" Papa said, still in his stern voice.

Hughie was startled. Was it so easy to see? Then her brothers and sisters began to laugh. They said together in a singsong voice, "Hughie pushed poor Grandma out of bed!"

Hughie grinned too. Her secret was still safe. She hung her head in mock shame and said,"Um-hmm. Every night when the clock struck twelve. She left because she was afraid of what I'd do on New Year's Eve!"

That started everyone talking about the unusual celebration just ahead. It was still the main subject when, with the kitchen work finished, the family gathered around the Christmas tree in the front parlor. The mica window in the door of the tall iron and nickel heating stove glowed orange, light that made the tinsel on the tree sparkle.

"Please, Papa, will you light the candles again?" Nora begged.

"I'll light them for one last time on New Year's Eve as part of our celebration," Papa said.

Mama had taken her favorite chair, beside the table with the kerosene lamp with the flowers painted on the shade. She had her mending basket on her lap and was pushing the darning egg into one of Papa's woolen socks, ready to weave wool thread back and forth over a hole in the heel. "The tree will have to come down on New Year's Day, before the ice crew boss turns this room back into his office," she said.

Hughie sighed. The ice crew! It was interesting to have them around, but it sure was a lot of work. And she'd have to watch out for that Cass. Last year he'd pinned her against the dining room wall and tried to kiss her, but one of the other men came into the room and he quickly jumped back. She'd make sure he was not around when she went in to set the table this year.

That night, deep in her feather bed, with the heavy quilts pulled around her shoulders, Hughie's last thought was that she had to be awake when Papa got up.

CHAPTER *4

It was still dark when Hughie opened her eyes and remembered her plan to go out and hunt for her locket. Yes, Papa was up. The room was icy cold, and she had to force herself to push aside the warm covers and get up. She pulled her flannel robe tightly about her and tiptoed across the cold floor to the window to see if dawn's gray light would soon be there.

"Oh, no!" she whispered.

Fresh snow was heaped around the windowpane, and more was blocking the view in a white curtain. No use going to look for the locket now! She turned and went back to curl up in the warmth of her bed. How would she ever find it? She was still worrying when she dropped off to sleep in spite of herself.

Mama called her an hour later. When she was dressed, she looked out the front window. Papa's footprints out to the road were only dimples in the white covering, but the snowstorm had ended.

When everyone had finished breakfast, she went out to Barney with the old bowl full of table scraps from last night's supper and bits of toast the smaller children had left on their breakfast plates. The sun, climbing in an azure sky, made the snow sparkle. Nora and Beth's snow family had taken on the look of white tepees, and the fort walls had grown eight inches higher.

At the smell of the pork chop and scraps and bones, Barney pushed aside the old piece of burlap that kept some of the cold wind out of his house, but his way was blocked by a wall of snow. Hughie set the food bowl off to one side and brushed the heaped-up snow away. As she picked up the bowl again, Barney crawled out of his house, stretched, and shook himself. Hughie held the bowl high and reached out a mittened hand to pat his head.

"Poor old Barney," she said. "Did you nearly freeze last night?" In answer, Barney bounced about in the deep snow and barked. She gave him his food, and as he ate she looked out over the lake. No longer could one see the silver of the icy surface. The lake wore a white blanket.

No chance of finding my locket now, she thought. She added aloud, "What'll I do?"

"You can help me carry in firewood, for one thing."

It was Jim. She hadn't heard his footsteps in the snow.

"No, thanks. I have enough chores of my own." She petted Barney again. The dog looked up appreciatively, licked his chops, and returned to his bowl.

Mrs. Riley, well bundled up, came from the cowshed. In the cold air, steam rose from the warm milk in the pail she carried.

"Br-r-r-r," She shuddered. "My hands will be frozen to this pail handle if I don't get inside. Come on, Hughie. We have lots to do."

Hughie had scarcely a minute to rest until lunchtime. She put the milk into shallow pans for the cream to separate for butter making, peeled apples for pies, and then, when the pies were in the oven, went up to the dormitory with her mother to sweep out the big room.

Only two of the twenty beds up there were in regular use, Jim's and Marty's.

"When the boys come in from chopping wood, they can move their things downstairs," Mama said. "They'll use Nora and Beth's room while the ice crew is here. Hughie, you'll have to share your bed with your sisters, like you did last year."

"Ugh!" Hughie said. She shivered from the cold air in the dormitory and shivered again at the thought of room sharing. "Nora and Beth kick me in their sleep. I'll probably have to sleep on the floor." She sighed.

"Hughie! That's enough of that kind of talk."

When Mama went downstairs to start the noon meal, Hughie was left alone in the long room with its two rows of beds. She leaned on her broom for a moment and watched dust particles in a shaft of sunlight coming through a small dormer window. She felt tired just thinking about all the work still ahead of them.

"Someday I'll have a maid to do this kind of stuff," she said aloud as she returned to the sweeping. Soon the dustpan had been emptied into an old bucket for the last time and she could return to the warm kitchen.

"I'm sure tired, Mama," she said.

Her mother touched her shoulder as she passed her with a plate of bread to put onto the table. The boys were already sitting down at their places. "Thank you, Hughie dear," Mama said. "I don't know how I'd get along without you. But I have good news for both of us. When the men come, Minnie will be here to help me. The boys went over to her house with the message that I need her, and she said she'd be here for sure."

Minnie was a neighbor who lived on a farm a half mile away. She had worked as Mrs. Riley's hired girl the last time the ice crew came. She came in the morning, stayed each day to clean up after the evening meal, and then hurried home to her husband.

"I'm sure glad to hear that, Mama, 'cause I'll be back in school and you can't do everything by yourself."

When they'd had a hot lunch and Rose was put in bed for her nap, Hughie and the boys went outdoors. Mama had given them two hours of free time, and somehow Hughie's tiredness disappeared.

"Too cold for packing snowballs and too much snow for skating," Jim decided.

They walked toward the lakeshore, passing the Knickerbocker Ice Company's storage building. It was almost empty now, but soon it would be refilled with new ice the crew would cut from Lake Monona. The icehouse was a huge wooden building, three hundred feet long and about half as wide. Its walls were double, with a two-foot space between them, filled with sawdust for insulation. At the end nearer the house there was a lower addition, not insulated, for stabling horses and storing tools.

As they walked past the building, it sheltered the three Rileys from the strong northwest wind. But as they reached the lakeshore the wind almost blew them out onto the ice. Hughie pulled her stocking cap down over her ears, turned up her coat collar, and wrapped her scarf around her throat. The air sparkled with blowing snow as they gazed southward over the lake.

"The wind is sweeping some of the snow away," she said. "Why don't we get the iceboat ready so we can use it as soon as the ice clears a little? Want to?"

"Might's well," Jim agreed.

The three of them walked back to the ice company's machinery storage shed. Their homemade iceboat was leaning against the outside wall, next to the railroad track. There had been a pile of old wood and metal pieces left from the building of the icehouse, piled there. In the fall of 1898, their mother showed them how they could build an iceboat, mostly from the scrap material.

"Like the one my brothers made when I was a girl," Mrs. Riley had said. She was handy at fixing things, such as broken boards on the porch steps, hinges that didn't work right, and skate blades that were dull. Papa never seemed to have time, and, besides, he was all thumbs, as Mama put it.

"The ice company doesn't want this junk," Mama had said. "I heard Mr. Owens say he wanted it cleared away. We can make a fine iceboat. Here's some good boards for the hull, and look at those bolts. We just need to clean off the rust."

They'd all worked then, sawing out three runners and the other pieces. Mrs. Riley took down the jar where she put the money she got from selling butter to the summer people who had cottages around Lake Monona. Mama's butter was kept in the icehouse and was the best butter in Madison, people said. With a little of her butter money, they'd been able to buy the few things they couldn't make from the scrap pile.

They'd used metal pieces from a broken sled for the

two runners attached to a crossboard at the front of the iceboat. The blacksmith up the road shaped a metal strip to fit the main runner for the stern. This runner was also the rudder and had a tiller attached to steer the boat. The sail was made from a well-patched old sheet. When they were ready to use the boat, they attached the sail to a pole that was used in the summer to prop up the clothesline.

They hadn't had a chance to use the boat this year. Their parents forbade them to take it onto the lake until Papa felt it was safe, for fear the wind would sweep the boat out onto thin ice.

Now the ice crew was coming in a few days. That meant two things, one good and one not so good. The ice was at least a foot thick—that was the good news. But soon a large part of the lake would be marked off from their use because there would be open water where the ice had been cut and removed. Iceboating season was short, unless they carried their boat far from the cutting area.

Jim was examining the edges of the runners that would contact the ice. "The blades have some rust on them" he said. "If we each sand and wax one we'll have the boat ready in a hurry."

Armed with pieces of emery cloth and sandpaper, a chunk of beeswax, and some old cloth rags, all three went to work. Barney came out to be with them. The work was almost finished when he barked and ran toward the road in front of the house. But his barking soon stopped, and in a moment he came bounding back alongside Jerry Byrnes.

"Hey, Rileys! Think it'll go in all this snow?"

Jim nudged Hughie with his elbow. "Here comes your boyfriend, Hughie."

"Shut up, Jim, he'll hear you," she muttered. Her cheeks were redder than the cold had made them as she turned to say hello to Jerry.

Marty answered Jerry's question. "No, but we're going to be ready when the wind clears the ice."

"My brother Will's boat is still in our barn. I'd race you with it, but he's off at college and I don't have anyone to be my crew. My little sister's no good at handling the sail." His sister was Nora's age.

Hughie kept on rubbing her runner blade, wanting to offer to crew for Jerry but afraid to say so. Marty unwittingly came to her rescue.

"We've got a sister that's big enough," he said. "We'll sell you Hughie."

That was more than Hughie could take. "*Sell* me? Oh, no, you don't! I'm not for sale, Smarty Marty!" She stood, hands on hips, eyes blazing. "And if that's the way you feel, you can work on this boat by yourselves!"

Jerry said, " 'Atta girl, Hughie! You tell 'em!"

Her shyness gone, Hughie turned and faced him. Jerry was grinning so widely that his gray stocking cap began to roll up, baring his ears to the cold wind. His blue eyes sparkled above the freckles that hadn't faded away since summer. A little of his red hair showed around the cap.

He pulled the cap back down to cover his ears. "How about it, Hughie? Will you be my crew? We'll show these brothers of yours how to win an iceboat race!"

Hughie could feel her cheeks burning even in the cold, and her heart pounded with excitement. To be

Jerry's crew! She swallowed hard and said, "We sure will, Jerry. We can practice tomorrow afternoon if the snow clears off enough."

"And have our race on New Year's Day," Jerry added.

"Great!"

Jim hadn't said anything through this. He'd counted on having Hughie for his crew. She was almost as old and big as Jerry. Marty wasn't nearly as strong or as experienced.

He said now, "Hughie, you'd better check that with Mama. Iceboating is for boys, not girls."

"Jim, you know Mama used to go iceboating when she was a girl! She won't mind. And who says it's just for boys, anyway?"

"Hughie's not like most of those prissy girls at school," Jerry put in. "She's more like another boy. That's why I asked her. She'd be almost as good as a brother."

Hughie felt like a balloon with the air escaping. She'd been hoping that Jerry felt about her as she did about him, not as he would feel about a sister—or, worse yet, a brother!

He went on. "Oh, hey—I really came over to tell you I've got a job with the ice crew. There was an ad in the paper for a boy to tend the horses, and they hired me. Every afternoon, after school, I'm to come and clean the stalls and do stuff like that. I'm supposed to start as soon as the horses get here."

The ice company owned sturdy horses that pulled ice delivery wagons through the Chicago streets during the warm months. In the winter, a few of them were brought out in railroad freight cars to pull snowplows and other implements needed for the ice-cutting work.

Hughie tried to hide the light, happy feeling that came at hearing that Jerry would be around every day. "That's nice," she said. She looked away from him and rubbed her mittens together to remove some icy bits of snow.

Jim and Marty were not afraid to show their enthusiasm. "That's great, Jerry!" Jim said. "Wish I was old enough for the job."

Marty added, "Hey, Jerry, maybe we can help, huh?"

Just then Mrs. Riley called, "Hughie! Time to come in."

Hughie felt a bit relieved to be called away. As she turned toward the house, she called back, "You two put the stuff away before you come in. And next time don't count on me to help you. Remember, I'm just a girl, and girls don't go iceboating!"

With faithful Barney at her heels, she tossed her braids back and strode along, head up. When she started up the porch steps, she looked back again to call in what she hoped was a casual tone, "See you tomorrow if the weather's right, Jerry!"

CHAPTER *5

The next day, Friday, brought gray skies, a strong wind, and a slight warming, but there was still too much snow on the lake for iceboating. After she fed Barney, Hughie went out onto the ice for another quick search for her locket. Again, no glimpse of the glint of gold.

The day passed in preparing for the coming of the ice crew. Hughie washed and dried long-unused dishes and wooden-handled steel knives and forks. She churned the cream, packed the fresh butter into small crocks, and covered each with several layers of cheesecloth, tied in place with string. In the afternoon, Jim and Marty pulled a sled to the general store to bring home eggs, yeast cakes, and a hundred-pound sack of flour for the baking still to come. Hughie and her mother baked cookies, filling the kitchen with a wonderful aroma and packing the cookies away in crock after crock.

Three kinds had been baked when Mr. Riley arrived home from work. "Enough to feed an army," he said when he saw the full crocks.

"By Tuesday, this place will be like an army camp," Mama said. "They'll go so fast we'll be baking more by the end of the week."

*   *   *

Saturday morning, when Hughie went out to feed Barney, the air had a different feel. The wind was from the south and the sky was clear.

"Hey, Barn, this should be a good day for iceboating." She put the bowl down on a place where the grass was showing through the snow. "Don't worry. We won't make you pull the boat like we did last year." Barney gave her a quick glance, as if he understood and was relieved, and then concentrated on eating his food.

"Hughie!" Mrs. Riley was calling from the back porch. "Don't take off your coat. I'm bringing out the men's blankets for airing. I want you to put up the clothesline and hang them out so they don't smell so strong of mothballs."

"Yes, Mama. But do you think maybe we can have time for iceboating this afternoon? We need to practice for the race on New Year's Day."

Mrs. Riley considered this a moment. "Yes, I think we're about ready, dear. I'll be baking more bread this afternoon, but I won't need your help with that. We'll get the beds for the crew made up while the blankets are airing."

Hughie fastened the clothesline to a hook on a back-porch post and walked to the cowshed, unwinding the rope as she walked. There was a hook on a corner post of the shed and she looped the line over it, snugged it up, and knotted it. Soon she had the first blankets of the stack over the line and blowing in the wind.

"Hey, Jim, I need the mast from the *Flash* to keep these blankets off the ground!" she called out. *Flash* was the name they'd proudly painted on their iceboat.

When Jim brought the mast-turned-clothes prop, he

said, "Looks like the lake is cleared enough for iceboating today."

Hughie, flinging another blanket over the line, called over her shoulder, "Looks better, doesn't it? You and Marty ready to take a beating from Jerry and me when we race on Monday?"

"Huh!" Jim snorted. "Don't hold your breath! You know our iceboat is a good one."

"Yes, but you won't have me for crew," Hughie said. "That's what you get for making fun of me."

"You just wait and see, Hughie," Jim said. "Marty'll do fine. We'll win that race. But you better get those blankets aired. We're going to need the mast so we can practice today." He went back to where he'd been splitting firewood. Hughie ran the line from the cowshed hook to a tree when the first span was filled with spread-out blankets. Soon the yard was crisscrossed with ropes, brown blankets waved in the wintry breeze, and Hughie went inside to help her mother make up the men's beds.

By afternoon, the wind had risen even more. The blankets had been taken inside and put on the beds before lunch, and the clothespole was no longer needed. Jim and Marty decided they'd work on the *Flash* some more, getting the mast and sail set for a practice run. The younger girls were staying indoors to make paper dolls out of fashion figures cut from a two-year-old Sears, Roebuck catalog, so Hughie was free. It was a good chance to look for her locket again.

This time she took with her the old back-porch broom, worn lopsided from much use, as she walked out onto the ice, Barney at her heels. When she was quite sure she was at the place where she and Jim had been scuffling on Wednesday afternoon, she began to poke about carefully, sweeping away the covering on the ice, always watching for a glint of gold. Much of the new snow had already been carried away by the wind.

Barney bounced around like a puppy, trying to get her to play and grabbing at the broom.

"Barney! Let go! Scoot,now. I've got to hunt some more," she said.

She didn't hear the faint swish of skate blades approaching.

"Hello, crew! What're you tryin' to do, sweep all the snow off the lake?"

It was Jerry. Hughie turned quickly, pushing back her braids. Jerry came to a skidding stop.

"Oh—Jerry. Just looking for something."

"For what? Maybe I can help."

"Well, promise if I tell that you won't blab it to Jim and Mart?"

"Cross my heart."

"I'm trying to find the locket my grandma gave me for Christmas. It came off out here, before the snowstorm."

Jerry looked at her questioningly. "How come?"

"I—I think it got caught in my scarf when I was out here and maybe fell onto the ice." She couldn't tell him she was fighting with Jim. Smiling at him, she added, "I just hafta find it."

"Well, let's hunt for it."

The two of them were still searching five minutes later, with no success, when they saw Marty and Jim coming.

Hughie dropped the broom, hoping they wouldn't notice it. "Don't tell them I lost my locket. Please."

"All right, if you don't want me to." Jerry began to do a figure eight, skating backward in the cleared area. "Out of my way, Barney!"

"What're you two doin' out there?" Jim called. He and Marty were pushing their iceboat out from the shore.

"Can't you see?" Jerry replied. "Clearing off a place so I can show Hughie how to do a figure eight."

Marty said, "But she doesn't have her skates on."

"That's even better when you're trying to learn how to do it backward. Isn't that right, Hughie?" As he spoke, he shoved off again to demonstrate the movement.

Hughie watched. "Yeah. Saves falling down so easy." She imitated Jerry's motions as best she could without skates, but Barney kept getting in her way. She said, "Thanks, Jerry. I'll try it with skates on next time."

Jim said, "We're gonna try the boat farther out where the ice shows through."

"Hey, Hughie, we should do that too," Jerry said. "Gotta practice for the big New year's Day race. Get your skates and skate back up to my place."

Hughie picked up the broom and headed for shore. "Be right back!"

In a few minutes she returned, carrying her skates. They had been a Christmas present a year ago—the newest kind of "club skates," with leather heel straps and steel clamps to hold the skates firmly over the edges of her shoe soles at the toe ends.

She called out to Jerry, "Mama said I can have two

hours but then she'll need me again. So we'll have to hurry.'' She reached the edge of the ice and got down on her right knee to put on her left skate. A minute later she had fastened the buckle on the strap of the right skate, too, and moved onto the ice.

''You stay here, Barney,'' she ordered as the big dog started to follow her. Barney stopped where he was, looking wistfully after Hughie. Skating was her favorite sport, and she struck out with long, strong strokes. She passed Jerry, who was watching the boys placing the sail on the *Flash*.

''Let's go, Jerry!'' she called and skated out where the snow was thinner to head toward Jerry's home, the next house along the lakeshore toward Madison. Jerry was soon sweeping along behind her, skating with strokes even longer than hers.

The Byrnes family had a boathouse that reached out over the water in summer but was now solidly set in ice. Jerry's iceboat, a stern-steerer like the Riley boat, was pushed onto the slope alongside the boathouse. It was not homemade like the Rileys' but had been purchased ready-built.

The name *Skimmer* was painted in dark blue on the slate-gray body of the iceboat, and there were two small leather-covered seats. Hughie, as crew, would sit on the one at the front crossbar. Her job would be to control the lines, the slender ropes with which the sail could be turned to catch the wind to get the most speed. Jerry would handle the tiller at the stern.

''I waxed the blades yesterday,'' he said. ''She's ready to pull out onto the ice.''

As the two of them moved the rather clumsy craft

from the shore out to open ice, Jerry asked, "Hughie, why do you want to keep it a secret about losing your locket and chain? Jim and Marty could help you look for it."

"No, one of them would be sure to tell Mama, and she'd be angry at me 'cause I wore it when she told me not to. She might even tell Grandma that I lost it, and it was a real special gift from her. Grandpa gave it to her before they were married."

"Your mother'll find out you lost it anyway, won't she?"

"Gee, I hope not! I think I'll find it soon. It's got to be somewhere near where we were looking. Will you keep an eye out for it, too?" They had the boat far enough out on the ice by this time, and Hughie helped unlash the sail as she went on. "When the top snow melts down out there in the sunshine, I'm sure it'll show up. But I've got to find it before the ice crew clears the snow away, and they'll be starting in a few days."

Jerry pulled the sail up and handed the lines to Hughie. "I think we're ready, Hughie. Let's get started. Hop on when we have her moving a bit and watch the sail for wind. Do you know how to tack?" Tacking was moving the sail so it would fill with wind on the other side, to change the boat's course.

Hughie gave her braids a toss. " 'Course I do. How else could I crew?"

Soon the wind filled the sail. "Okay, hop on now!" Jerry called out, and Hughie climbed aboard. Jerry took his seat too, as the wind kept the boat moving. In a moment they were skimming along nicely.

The next hour passed quickly. At the tiller, Jerry

called out commands as he turned the runners to carry them southwestward, parallel with the shore. They went about a quarter mile and then turned to cross the lake, following the course usually used in races between small iceboats. Hughie felt thankful that she knew enough about tacking to catch the wind at each turn without much time wasted.

When they had completed the turn, Hughie looked back and saw her brothers in the *Flash* following the same course they were taking.

"Hey, Jerry! Jim and Marty have the *Flash* moving along pretty good!"

Jerry turned to see the Riley boat gliding smoothly. "Gee, I didn't think a little homemade boat could move that fast," he said. "Might not be as easy to beat them as I thought it would be."

Hughie felt proud of her family's skill in boatbuilding and at the same time needed to make her brothers sorry they had lost her help. "Yeah. The *Flash* really is a good little iceboat," she said. Then, remembering Marty's insulting offer to sell her help to Jerry, she added, "Let's widen the gap between us." She pulled the sail to catch the wind a little better, and *Skimmer* lived up to her name.

" 'Atta boy!" Jerry shouted.

Hughie smiled back at him, deciding to ignore being called a boy and take it as a compliment.

They were about to pass by the icehouse as they headed toward Jerry's home when Barney, waiting patiently at the lake's edge, saw them coming. He bounded out, racing to reach them.

"Turn the rudder, Jerry!"

Jerry turned the boat just in time to avoid a collision.

Hughie shouted, "Barney, stay out of the way!"

Barney, hearing the disapproval in Hughie's voice, pulled back a bit and then trotted along behind the iceboat. Soon they had beached it and Hughie was putting her skates back on as best she could between Barney's welcoming kisses.

"We'll beat them easy," she said. "Day after tomorrow, Jerry! And Happy New Year!"

"Same to you, Hughie. You *are* just as good as a brother!"

CHAPTER *6

"Ow!"

Hughie had been awakened by a kick in her back. Beth, sleeping between Hughie and Nora, was the kicker. Still sound asleep, the little girl rolled onto her back and flung her right arm across Hughie's face.

Hughie pushed the arm down and tried to go to sleep again. But she could hear the sound of ashes being shaken down in the kitchen range and knew that Mama was already up.

"I'm going back to sleep. This is Sunday," she muttered. And then suddenly she was wide awake. *This was the last day of 1899—and the very last day of the nineteenth century!*

She glanced out the window. The sky was the gray of early morning.

I want to remember this day forever, she thought.

The whole family had had their Saturday night baths in the kitchen the night before. One advantage Hughie had as the eldest was to be allowed to use the washtub of hot water first, before Jim and Marty. The water had to be heated on the range, so three tubfuls had to do for the whole family, with Mama and Papa sharing the last one.

Hughie got her clean woolen union suit from the dresser drawer. It felt good to pull the warm underwear close around her and button it all the way to the top. She hooked her black elastic garters through the tabs at the waist at each side and closed the safety pin tops. Next she rolled down one of her best black mercerized cotton stockings and pulled it over her right foot. Then came the tricky part—folding the extra width of the knitted underwear leg into a smooth wedge before pulling the stocking over it. With one stocking unrolled all the way up, she fastened the garter tab and repeated the performance for her left leg.

Mama made her wear a growing girl's corselet on Sundays, now that she was thirteen, but she would put that and her petticoat on later, when she put on her Sunday dress. For now, she just needed to get ready for that cold morning trip down the path, so she put on her everyday shoes and her warm robe.

"Morning, Hughie," Mama said. "You're up early."

"Mama, don't you remember? This is a *very* special day! New Year's Eve, 1899! When midnight comes the eighteen hundreds will be gone forever."

By the time she'd said all that, Hughie was out in the back storeroom, pulling her coat on over her bathrobe and her galoshes over her shoes. Outside, it was still so cold and gray that Barney didn't even bother to come out of his house as she went by. A few minutes later she was back in the warm kitchen.

"Oh, Mama! I want to remember every minute of this day!"

Mrs. Riley was shaping sausage patties for breakfast. She had biscuits ready to go into the oven as soon as it was hot enough to make them rise.

"It *is* a special day," she agreed. She sat down at the

table. "You know, Hughie, I've been thinking about the wonderful things that have been invented in the thirty-seven years I've been alive. When I was fourteen years old, in 1876, there was a great fair in Philadelphia. It was for the hundredth birthday of the United States."

"Mama! Did you go to it?"

Mrs. Riley shook her head. "No, dear. We were too far away, here in Wisconsin. But I saw pictures in a magazine. There were huge machines for factories and new farm machines for horses to pull. And Alexander Graham Bell was there with his brand-new invention."

"The telephone! I wish we had one, Mama."

"Now just who would you call, Hughie? But maybe someday . . ."

Hughie's eyes were dreamy. "Let's buy an automobile, Mama. Papa can crank it up and away we'll go!"

Mrs. Riley sighed and then got up to test the oven's heat. As she put the biscuits in to bake, she turned to Hughie and smiled. "Yes, honey. I can just see your papa all dressed up in a checkered suit, sitting in one of those horseless carriages Mr. Olds is building. He'd squeeze the horn bulb, and everyone would get out of the way."

They both laughed. "I can see him too, Mama. He'd really make the dust fly! That's what we'll do in the twentieth century, won't we?"

Just then Papa came into the kitchen, pulling his suspenders over his long-sleeved undershirt. "What's going on out here?"

"The twentieth century, Papa! Mama's talking to Grandma on the telephone, and I'm going for a ride on a trolley—and you're sitting in one of Mr. Olds's automobiles, just driving along like crazy. Happy New Century, Papa!"

At half past nine o'clock, all the Rileys except Mama and baby Rose were walking the mile to church, bundled up in heavy coats over their best suits and dresses. The snow sparkled in the sun and crunched under their feet, for it had turned clear and colder in the night. All of them, even Papa, had rosy cheeks when they got there.

Jerry was sitting near the back of the church with his parents, Dr. and Mrs. Byrnes. Hughie pretended not to see him as the Rileys walked farther up the aisle to where the pews were not yet filled, but she felt her cheeks glowing.

When the service ended the Rileys were among the last to leave the building. Hughie wished Papa wouldn't take so long. Jerry and his folks would already be in their sleigh, she was sure. But she and the boys had to walk behind Papa, who held Nora's and Beth's mittened hands as they went carefully down the snow-covered stone steps.

As soon as it was safe to look around, Hughie was glad to see that the Byrneses were still there. In fact, Jerry seemed to be watching for the Rileys. He called out, "Hey, Hughie! C'mere! Got something to tell you!"

Hughie went over to where Jerry was standing with his parents.

"Hello, Hughie," Mrs. Byrnes said. "Jerry tells me you're going to be his crew in a race tomorrow, and we thought you'd like to be in on some fun tonight too."

"We're having a New Year's Eve hayride, just for the

big kids around here," Jerry said. "You're invited, Hughie. Can you come?"

Hughie's heart beat wildly. Jerry took some of the joy away when he added, "Ask your father. Julie Schultz and some other girls will be there too."

Julie was the prettiest girl in the eighth grade, and she had her eye on Jerry. She was always talking about "my friend Jerry Byrnes"—like she owns him, Hughie thought.

Hughie'd never been invited to a nighttime party before. She hurried over to where her father stood talking to another man and tugged at his sleeve.

"Papa, I'm invited to a New Year's Eve hayride and a party at the Byrneses. Can I go? Please, Papa?"

Mr. Riley looked thoughtful. "Are the boys invited too?"

"No, Papa. It's just for big kids."

"You're too young to be out late at night without your brothers, Hughie."

"Oh, Papa, this is such a special night! Please!"

Dr. Byrnes came walking over. "Riley, we'll look after your girl and see that she gets safely home right after midnight."

"I don't want anything to happen to her, Doc. Some roughnecks from the ice company crew are already in town."

"She'll be safe, Mr. Riley. I'll see to it."

"Well, all right then."

Hughie hurried over to Jerry. "Papa said yes!"

"Great! We'll come by about nine o'clock, or maybe half past. You'll hear the sleigh bells jingle," Jerry said. "After the hayride, we'll go to my house to see the New

Year and the new century in. There's cider and doughnuts—and we saved a big bunch of firecrackers from
the Fourth of July. We'll set them off at midnight."

Hughie tried to hide her excitement. "I'll be ready,
Jerry." She turned to go back to where Papa was trying
to keep the two little girls from escaping his grip on
their mittened hands.

"See you tonight!" Jerry called, and hurried off to the
small sleigh where his father and mother and little sister
were already sitting. The mare was tossing her head
impatiently.

At home, Hughie's mind was on the evening ahead
as she helped her mother with dinner: fried chicken
with mashed potatoes, dumplings, and gravy, the usual
Sunday menu.

While they were taking their seats and the food was
being passed, Mrs. Riley glanced at the neckline of
Hughie's dress.

Finally she said what was on her mind. "Hughie,
you're dressed up for Sunday. Why aren't you wearing
the lovely locket Grandma gave you?"

This was the moment Hughie had been dreading.
Should she tell her mother the truth? She wanted to,
and yet when she opened her mouth the words would
not come. She pretended to choke a bit in the awkward
silence, gulped down some milk, wiped her mouth
with her napkin as she had been taught to do, and
finally said, "Mama, the locket and necklace are so nice
I don't want anything to happen to them. So I didn't
wear them today. They could fall off and be lost in the
snow! And I certainly don't want to wear them on a
hayride."

She could feel a wave of warmth flooding her neck and cheeks. Marty noticed it too. "Hughie's blushing 'cause she's going to her boyfriend's party! Look how red she is!"

Jim chimed in. "I'll say! Boy, she's red as a beet!"

For once, Hughie didn't mind their teasing. Mama seemed to have accepted her excuse about the locket. Hughie was glad she hadn't told the boys about losing it, for they would surely have used this moment to tell Mama. And I didn't really tell a lie, she thought. *But it was just the same as a lie,* a little voice inside her said.

When the dishes were washed and dried, Hughie decided to go out to look for her locket again. On Sundays, the Riley children were allowed to go for walks, but not to skate or have snowball fights or play games.

Hughie saw her chance to go out alone. Usually, Nora and Beth would have begged her to pull them on a sled as she walked, but this afternoon they joined little Rose in napping so they could stay awake for the coming of the New Year.

The rest of the family was in the warm kitchen. The boys had Christmas gift sets of thirty lead soldiers, with little cannons and guns. They were busily arranging them for battle on the linoleum-covered floor. Papa was in the platform rocker, with the Madison Sunday newspaper over his eyes. Mama, for once, was sitting with her eyes closed and her hands idle in her lap.

"I'm going for a walk," Hughie announced. Not even Mama seemed to hear. Hughie slipped out quietly.

With Barney at her heels, she went out onto the ice.

This time she did not take a broom, thinking that perhaps she'd swept away the locket without seeing it.

"Come on, Barney. Help me find that locket," she said. Soon the two of them were making the snow fly, Barney with his paws and Hughie with her mittened hands as she knelt on the ice. They searched so long she was chilled to the bone, as Mama would say. It was very discouraging. She decided she'd have to give up for today. Maybe tomorrow—

She was getting to her feet when she heard Barney give a low growl. He turned to face the icehouse and sniffed the air.

"What's the matter with you, Barney?" she asked. Then even Hughie caught a new scent. Horses! Faintly, she could hear the occasional stamping of a hoof on the wooden floor of the stable, and once she thought she heard a male voice. If the first men were already here and the horses being moved in, she didn't have much time left to hunt. Maybe she'd better keep on searching.

Barney's growl was louder. A man was coming out the door at the stable end of the icehouse.

Hughie had a sudden feeling that she couldn't breathe. It was that man, Cass. Barney barked and rushed up to him.

"Get away from me!" Cass yelled. He swore and kicked Barney. The dog pulled back, then snarled and moved toward the man again, but cautiously this time.

"Barney! No! Come back here, Barney!" Hughie ran to the shore. As soon as she reached the dog, she hooked her mittened hand around his collar and tugged to pull him away. But it was all she could do to hold him. Again Barney snarled and tried to get at Cass.

"Easy now, Barney. It's all right," she said softly and stroked the dog's head to quiet him as Cass backed off a few steps. At last Barney seemed satisfied, turned away from Cass, and stood panting beside Hughie.

Cass spat tobacco juice, staining the untracked snow alongside the icehouse. "That's more like it," he said. "You keep that mutt away from me, miss. Tie him up." Then, as he looked at Hughie, his eyes brightened. "Well, if it ain't the little miss from the icehouse family. You sure growed up since I seen you last."

Hughie had been taught to be polite. "Hello, Mr. Cass," she said.

"Just Cass, honey."

"I have to go now," Hughie said, still holding Barney's collar. "Come on, Barney." She started back toward home, Barney close beside her.

"I'll be seein' you, missy," Cass called after her.

Hughie kept on walking, pretending not to have heard. "I hope not," she muttered. She added, "I don't like him any more than you do, Barney. I'm glad you went after him, even if you have been taught not to do that to the ice crew."

Back in the house, Hughie said nothing about her encounter with Cass, thinking that Mama might ask her what she was doing out on the lake. She shuddered. She couldn't forget the way he'd looked at her.

CHAPTER * 7

Soon, Hughie knew, she'd hear the jingle of the sleigh bells and it would be time to go to the New Year's Eve party. She was wearing her best school outfit, dark blue wool in sailor style, and had even dabbed on a bit of Grandma's cologne. She'd brought her coat, scarf, cap, and mittens in from the cold back storeroom to warm them up in the parlor. Her galoshes stood ready too.

Now she felt a bit fidgety, listening for sounds from outdoors above the chatter of her sisters and brothers, gathered for the last lighting of the Christmas tree—and the family's last evening in the parlor until the ice crew left. The tree would come down in the morning, and the parlor would become the ice crew boss's office and sleeping room.

"Don't forget, Papa," Nora said, pulling at her father's sweater sleeve. "You promised to light the candles on the Christmas tree tonight."

"Yes, my little dove. I'm about to do just that. All of you stand back and watch. We don't want to set the tree afire." As he talked, he had been lighting an ordinary candle with a large match.

"Hurry, Papa!" Nora jumped up and down in excitement.

The candle nearest the top of the tree, a gold-colored one, was the first to glow in the darkened room. One by one, the other flames appeared, and with each one the children applauded. There were twenty-four candles in all—four inches long and about as thick as a pencil, blue, red, green, and gold, set into small holders clamped to the tree branches. As the candles glowed, the tinsel garlands sparkled with new life, and the glass ball ornaments were transformed into magical living worlds.

"Last candle," Papa said as he crouched to reach the lowest one on the tree.

"O Christmas tree, O Christmas tree, you stand in verdant beauty," Mama sang in her clear voice, and the children joined in. Hughie was so enchanted that she forgot to listen for the jingling of sleigh bells. She was singing along with the rest when there was a shout from outside. "Hughie!"

She hurried into her outer clothes, quickly kissed her mother, and blew a kiss to her father, who stood keeping a watchful eye on the Christmas tree.

"Happy New Year! See you next century!" she called as she headed out into the night.

A team of sturdy chestnut-brown horses was hitched to a hay wagon on which sleigh runners had replaced the wheels. About a dozen boys and girls were seated on bales of straw along the sides of the wagon bed, with blankets covering their legs and feet. A few of them were older, but most were seventh- or eighth-graders.

"Hughie, hurry up! We're all freezing, waiting for you." Hughie recognized Julie Schultz's high-pitched voice.

Jerry was standing on the wagon at the back. "You're

the last one to be picked up," he said as he took her hands and pulled her up. "Move over, Julie, and make room for Hughie."

He turned toward the pretty blond girl who was sitting on the endmost straw bale on one side of the wagon.

"Oh, that's your place, Jerry."

"Come on, Julie. Move over. I'll sit at the end and keep you girls from falling out." Julie moved, but toward the end of the wagon, leaving room only for Jerry. Hughie walked past her and took the opened place.

As Jerry sat down, he called out, "All set now, Dad!" The horses stamped their feet and shook themselves, impatient to be moving.

On the driver's seat, Dr. Byrnes sat beside the farmer who owned the wagon and team. "Then let the party begin." And he called out, "All together, now—Happy New Year!" The shouted greeting was lusty and loud, as the team leaned into the harness and the sleigh bells rang.

Looking toward the window where the lighted tree glowed, Hughie saw her father wave as the sleigh began to move. For a moment she felt a pang of separation from her family. She was missing something special. But the next minute she was singing as lustily as the rest, "Dashing through the snow, in a one-horse open sleigh—"

The sleigh, with the bells ringing rhythmically, went southeast about a mile and a half along the snow-covered lakeshore road and then turned due east, going past widely separated farmhouses. There had been enough travel since the snowstorm that well-packed ruts, shining under a full moon, made a clear track for the horses to follow.

A quarter of a mile past the turn, they approached the crossing of the Chicago and Northwestern Railroad. The team had to slow down to make the steep rise to the tracks.

The long sleigh was at the top when the big fellow sitting beside Hughie yelled, "Away you go!" He gave her and the bale of straw a tremendous push—and over the open wagon end went Jerry, Julie, Hughie, and the bale, tumbling to the snowy road. The same thing happened to Tim Tompkins and Julie Schultz's older brother, Bill, who had been sitting across from them.

Amid shrieks and laughter from those still on the hay wagon, the five erstwhile riders and two straw bales were left behind. The driver kept the team pulling across the railroad tracks and down the slope on the eastern side.

Hughie found herself sliding along the road on her bottom, as did Jerry, Tim, Bill, and a shrieking Julie. Everyone except Julie got to their feet and stood laughing as they brushed snow and straw from their clothes.

"We look like a bunch of snowmen!" Jerry said.

"Snowmen stuffed with straw," Hughie added. Then they noticed that Julie was still sitting in the road, rubbing her right ankle.

"Come on, Julie," Jerry said. "We have to catch up with the sleigh."

Julie continued to sit. "I think my ankle is broken," she said.

"Oh, Julie, it can't be broken with your shoe and overshoe as protection. Here, I'll help you stand up."

Julie grasped Jerry's mittened hands but pulled so hard that he slipped and went down beside her. He got up and called to Julie's brother, "Hey, Bill, give me a hand." A moment later, Julie stood on one foot, with her arms over Jerry's and Bill's shoulders.

Three of the other sleigh riders appeared at the top of the slope on the railroad tracks. "Hey, you kids! Watcha doin' down there? You're s'posed to be on a sleigh ride!"

Hughie called up. "Tell that to those smarties who pushed us off!"

"Can't you walk at all, Julie?" asked Jerry. He and Bill were doing their best to get up the slippery slope.

"I'll try," Julie said in a small, weak voice. She stood on both feet. "Oh, it hurts!" she cried.

"All right," Bill said. "Hop on one foot. Come on, Jerry. Let's go."

Bill spoke for both boys as they half carried and half dragged his sister, slipping back almost as much as they went upward.

"For Pete's sake, Julie, why'd you have to do that? It's hard enough getting up this hill without carrying you too. Hughie fell off the wagon same as you, and she's not hurt."

"Hughie—she's just a tomboy," Julie said.

"You'd be more fun if you were more like her and not so prissy," Bill told her.

Tim noticed the two bales of straw, broken open now, lying in the middle of the road. "Hughie, we'd better push these bales off the road before we go on." This done, he said, "Race you up and over!" And Tim and

Hughie slipped and slid their way up the slope, getting to the top just ahead of Jerry, Bill, and Julie.

"The winner—Hughie Riley!" called out one of the boys who had been watching them as Hughie, panting, crossed the tracks first.

The sleigh was now stopped about fifty feet ahead. "Last one on is a big fat toad!" shouted one of those who hadn't jumped off. There was a mad scramble to get aboard, amid much laughter and playful shoving. Hughie found herself well forward on the sleigh this time, between Mary Schultz and Tim.

Julie and her escorts were last to reach the sleigh. Dr. Byrnes, waiting at the back, said, "Sit here, Julie, and let me check to see if you've done anything serious to that ankle."

The doctor removed her overshoe and unlaced her black kid shoe far enough to be able to feel the ankle joint. "Just a bit of a sprain. I don't even think it will swell much." Relacing the shoe, he said, "Keep the laces snug to hold the swelling down."

When Julie's overshoe was on and buckled, Jerry and Bill helped her slide safely back in the wagon bed and then sat down with their legs dangling over the end. As Dr. Byrnes took his seat beside the driver, he called back, "No more of that rough stuff, kids. Let's have some songs instead. How about 'Oh! Susannah'?"

Soon the boys and girls were singing heartily again. Most of the straw that had been neatly baled was now spread out in the bed of the wagon, and the riders sprawled comfortably. A few more miles and three sharp right turns—each of which brought shrieks from the girls as they found themselves thrown against their neighbors—and they were back at the road around Lake Monona. The sleigh swung to the right again and headed northward. There was a loud groan as it passed Blooming Grove School No. 3, where most of them would be going in two days.

"Let's sing 'School Days'!" someone called out.

"Let's not!" others yelled, but the song soon filled the air.

The singing continued as they approached the Riley house. Hughie knew the Christmas tree candles would have been snuffed out long ago, but she watched to see if a lamp still glowed in the front window. It did, and Mama, having heard the sound of the singing, pulled back the lace curtain and waved. A few minutes later, the sleigh pulled to a stop at the Byrneses' house.

Jerry and Bill jumped off and Jerry shouted, "Let's go inside! Second half of the party's about to begin!"

Everyone but Julie started up the walk. Julie stayed behind as the others left. To the one or two who offered her a hand, she said, "Jerry will help me in."

But Jerry was busy playing host, urging his guests toward the door, where his mother was welcoming them. His father was up front paying the driver, who wanted to take his horses to their deserved rest in the home barn. As Dr. Byrnes said, "Happy New Year, John!" and the sleigh was about to pull away, they heard a plaintive voice from the wagon bed.

"Jerry, I'm waiting for you to help me down!"

"John, hold the horses!" Dr. Byrnes shouted. He and Jerry put Julie between them, made a seat of their gloved hands, and carried her up the walk.

In a few minutes, Julie was in an armchair in the

Byrneses' warm parlor, where the guests were gathered. Hughie, like most of the others, sat in a circle on the flowered parlor rug. Soon they were all sipping hot mulled cider and munching freshly fried doughnuts.

"Forty minutes left of the nineteenth century!" Tim called out.

Jerry was passing out paper and pencils. "Everyone think of something that could happen in the twentieth century and write it down. Make it as wild as you want to—even something that seems impossible. But don't put your name on the paper. We'll mix them up and then each person will draw one to read aloud."

The room was quiet as the guests thought a moment and then began to write.

Jerry collected all the papers in a hat.

One of the girls drew first. " 'I'll build a flying machine and it will go all the way to Chicago before it comes down,' " she read. "Now that's a silly idea. Who ever heard of a machine that can fly?"

Jake Meiers said, "It's not so silly. People have been trying to build flying machines for a long time."

"Yeah, but they don't work. I mean a machine that will really fly for miles and miles!" said Tim.

"Hey, Tim, you gave yourself away. But I'll be there to watch when you go flying away." said Bill.

Then a really wild idea was read. " 'I am going to fly to the moon.' " Everyone hooted at the thought.

Julie was the next reader. "This could never come true," she said. "It says, 'I'll have a magic box on the table, and it will talk as clearly as a telephone, and it will play music for me.' "

Jerry said, "I don't think that's so impossible, Julie. It could come true. You're next, Hughie."

Hughie drew a paper from the hat, unfolded it, and read, " 'I'm going to have a magic lantern machine in my house that will show pictures of what is going on all over the world, while it is happening.' "

"Hey, who's the dreamer who thought that one up? Imagine sitting in your own house and seeing what's happening hundreds of miles away!"

"Well," said one of the older boys, "you can already hear voices from miles away on a telephone. Why not have cameras that will send pictures instantly?"

Jerry said, "I read about Thomas Edison showing pictures that make people look like they're moving. But it'll take more than one century for someone to invent a camera that will let us see pictures of what's happening somewhere far away while it's still going on!"

Hughie heard her own prophecy read next. " 'I will sit in a chair in a big flying machine and go all the way over the Atlantic Ocean to London in less than one day.' "

"Ha! That's impossible! It takes a steamship at least ten days to cross the Atlantic. How could *anything* get there in one day?"

"Who's to know what the twentieth century will bring?" Jerry said. He looked at the clock on the fireplace mantel. "Hey, kids—five minutes to go. Get your coats on so we can set off the firecrackers!"

There was a rush to the bedroom for coats, caps, and scarves, and then, with their overshoes back on, everyone but Julie followed Jerry out the door. A ringing of bells began, and they all knew that 1900 had come.

Dr. Byrnes was already outside to distribute firecrackers, with pieces of smoldering punk for lighting the fuses. Jerry hurried out to be the first to light one.

"Jerry, wait for me!" Julie called plaintively from the porch, where she stood with Mrs. Byrnes.

Jerry looked back impatiently. "Watch from there, Julie!" he called, and at the same time threw a lighted firecracker into the air to start the celebration. Bill's firecracker exploded next, and soon there were too many bangs to separate them. Up the street, people came outside and banged on dishpans, but no one made more noise than the young folks at the Byrneses' house. Firecrackers flared and exploded for five minutes, and then they were all gone, and it was quiet.

Jerry raised his arm. "One last greeting to the nineteen hundreds and then the party's over," he called out. "Ready? Happy Twentieth Century!"

Dr. Byrnes had harnessed Dolly, his black mare, to the cutter he used to make calls on his patients. The horse, accustomed to being put to work at any hour of the day or night, seemed to enjoy the jingle of her bells and snorted as she waited for passengers.

"Help Julie walk out here, Bill," Dr. Byrnes said. "Climb in, Mary. I'll take the Schultz family home first. Now, boys, let's see who is seeing each girl safely home." There were more boys than girls, and soon groups formed around each girl except Hughie. No one else lived between the Byrneses' and the Rileys'.

"Jerry, you walk with Hughie and make sure she gets home safely. Happy New Year, all of you!"

There was a chorus of voices—"Thanks, Dr. Byrnes!

Thanks, Mrs. Byrnes! Happy New Year!"—and the groups started for home.

"Good night, Julie, hope your ankle's better tomorrow," Jerry said as his father picked up the reins. "If it is, come over to the lake and watch Hughie and me win the iceboat race tomorrow afternoon."

"You and *Hughie?*" Julie paused, and her voice took on a whining tone. "I thought you'd come over to see me tomorrow afternoon. I don't think I'll be able to walk that soon."

"Won't have time, Julie. Gotta start workin' with the ice company horses after the race. 'Night, Bill, Mary." He waved as the sleigh started to move and then hurried to catch up with Hughie, who had walked about fifty feet toward home.

He took her arm. "Why do girls have to be waited on so much?"

Hughie pulled away. "Well, Mr. Jerry Byrnes, I can get home all right alone. You don't have to wait on *me!*"

Jerry took her arm again. "Hey, Hughie, I didn't mean you. I meant girls like Julie. You're more like one of us guys!"

CHAPTER *8

By early afternoon, right after the family's New Year's Day dinner, Jim and Marty had the *Flash* out on the ice. Hughie watched them get ready for the race as she waited for Jerry. She thought about the party and decided the cologne she'd put on was wasted. When he walked her home, Jerry had not acted as if he thought she needed any help over the slippery spots, though she was sure he helped Julie when he walked *her* home—even when Julie didn't have a sprained ankle.

He'd talked about the race and told her she'd better wear warm wool stockings and maybe a pair of Jim's knickers instead of a dress. Well, she hadn't done that. That would make him think of her as "one of the guys" more than ever. *Do I have to act prissy, like Julie, for him to think of me as a girl?*

"I'd rather die!" she muttered.

She hadn't noticed Jim standing close beside her.

"You'd rather die? Rather die than what, Hughie?"

"Rather die than be like some people I know," she answered.

"Like who?"

"Like *whom*," she corrected him. "It's none of your business, anyway. I was talking to myself."

Jim couldn't let that pass unnoticed. "You know what it means when you start talking to yourself, Hughie."

"Yes, it means there's nobody around I'd rather talk to."

The banter was interrupted by a shout from the west. Jerry was out on the ice, pushing his *Skimmer* toward the *Flash*. He motioned for Hughie to come and help him.

As she started running, Hughie called back, "So long, you two. We'll be back here in a few minutes for the start of the race. And we're going to win."

Barney thought it was playtime and in a moment was right at her heels. "Okay, Barney," she said, "you can come with me now, but when the race starts you've gotta stay home!"

Barney answered with a short bark and ran ahead toward *Skimmer.*

"She's ready, Hughie!" Jerry called out as his crew came near. "I've got the runner blades waxed and polished so she'll slide if you just blow on her. Let's get the sail up and ride her back to the starting line."

In a minute the sail was unfurled and they were ready to shove off. Hughie gave a running push and jumped on board, with Barney scampering alongside on the ice to keep up.

" 'Atta girl, Hughie!" Jerry called as he, too, got on board and the iceboat kept going smoothly. "We'll win this race!"

"I think we will—and I'm glad to hear you know I'm a girl!"

Looking back at Jerry, Hughie saw his wide grin growing wider. "Yeah, Hughie. I know you're a girl— but you're still almost as good as a brother!"

Hughie leaned over to scoop up some snow, causing *Skimmer* to swerve slightly.

"Watch it, crew—" Jerry was saying when the handful of snow hit him in the face. "Hey! Truce! We gotta work together."

They were quite close to the *Flash*, out on the ice in readiness for the race. Jerry and Hughie got off *Skimmer* to turn her around. In a moment, the two boats were lined up side by side, parallel to the shore, in a west-by-south direction. Barney ran excitedly back and forth in front of them.

"I'd better get Barney out of the way," Hughie said. She left *Skimmer*, took hold of the dog's collar, and walked partway to the shore with him. "Now you stay there, Barney," she said. "Be a good dog. Sit."

She was startled to hear a man's voice from the shore. "Need a starter for your race?"

She looked up quickly, glad to see it was the ice crew boss, not Cass. "Oh, hello, Mr. Owens. Will you start us off? That would be a big help."

"Be glad to, Miss Hughie," Mr. Owens said. They walked together back to where Jerry waited at the stern of the *Skimmer*, and Jim and Marty waited behind the *Flash*. Barney obediently sat where Hughie had left him.

"Hello, Mr. Owens," Jim and Marty said.

"Hello, boys. You've both grown a bit since last winter. And who is this young man?"

"I'm Jerry Byrnes, Mr. Owens." Jerry stepped forward. As Mr. Owens shook hands with him, he added, "And I guess you're my top boss. I'm the boy who was hired to clean the stable and tend the horses each evening."

"Well, Jerry Byrnes, I'm glad to meet you. Cass tells me you're to start this evening. He'll be your supervisor."

"I'll be on the job as soon as this race is finished and I take *Skimmer* home, Mr. Owens. I live at the first place to the west, so it won't take me long to get back."

"Fine," Mr. Ownes said. "Now let's check out the rules for this race. Have you agreed on markers for your course?"

"Yes, sir," Jim said. "The racers always use a big oak tree about three quarters of a mile from here as the first turn. It's just before the creek mouth—between the Madison city limit sign and the mouth of the creek. There's a boat mooring post out in the lake that we have to go around. Then we head southeast, crossing the lake." He pointed as he went on. "It's almost a mile to a buoy that sticks up through the ice. We have to pass the buoy before we start our turn."

Jerry chimed in. "After we go around the buoy, it's easy to see where we're heading. We just aim for the east end of the icehouse here."

Mr. Owens was getting the triangular course set in his mind. He said, "But suppose the two boats are neck and neck—prow and prow, let's say—in a real close race. There should be a definite line that marks the finish." He looked toward the south, along the course the boats would be following as they approached the finish. "You'll be heading right toward the icehouse. So let's set a straw bale on the ice here, far enough out to give you a safe stopping distance before you hit the shore.First one to pass it wins."

"Sounds good to me," Jerry said. "How about you, Jim?"

Jim nodded. "Okay with me."

"Agreed, then. You two captains shake hands and

take your positions. Cass and I'll bring the bale out as soon as you're on the way."

"Sure. Mr. Owens, will you be around to see who passes the bale first?" Jim asked.

"I promise to be here. May have to go inside and warm up a bit, but I'll be back out in plenty of time to judge the finish."

The two teams took starting positions, each person crouched over with hands on the craft, ready to push the boats for a good start on the first of the three legs of the course.

"On your mark—get set—*go!*" Mr. Owens called, and the four young people shoved off. Soon both Marty and Hughie were in their places on board, and a moment later Jerry and Jim were seated at the rudder positions.

The *Flash* was farther out from the shore and got off to a start so good she took the lead, with *Skimmer* close behind her. Marty was handling the sail, and when a puff of wind came, the *Flash* veered a little to the right, cutting in front of *Skimmer*.

"Hughie," Jerry called, "I'm going to pull a little to port—to the left—so we can get around them when we catch up. And be ready at the turn to reset the sail. We'll have this northwest wind right at our backs."

"Okay, Jerry. I know how to do it!"

The Riley boat held the lead until they neared the mooring post, when *Skimmer* pulled alongside. *Skimmer* was farther from the shore. Jerry saw that he would have to turn the rudder to take them to the right a bit— "starboard," boaters call it—in order to pass the post on the shore side as the rules demanded, allowing *Flash* to make the turn first. This put *Skimmer* behind *Flash* as they started the long run southeast.

"Come on, crew!" Jerry shouted to Hughie. "Grab those lines and let's pick up all the northwest wind we can!"

"Aye, aye, skipper!" Hughie called. "Watch us go now!" She had swung the sail into better position, and while Marty was still making his adjustments, *Skimmer* passed *Flash*.

" 'Atta boy, Hughie!" Jerry shouted. "We've got 'em chasing us now!"

Hughie was so intent on her part in handling the iceboat that she didn't even notice that Jerry had reverted to using "boy" instead of "girl." *Skimmer* held the lead, but the Riley boat, lighter in weight, picked up a little more speed and narrowed the gap between them.

Each moment took them closer to the buoy that marked the turn, with *Skimmer* still holding a slight lead. This time Jerry and Hughie could choose their course as they made the turn, leaving the Riley boys farther behind. For this last leg, heading almost directly into the wind, the crew had to tack again, and Hughie, with more experience, caught the wind faster than Marty did.

Jerry and Hughie still kept their advantage as the two boats headed for the icehouse. In the distance they could make out the figures of both Mr. Owens and Cass, and finally they could see the straw bale they must pass to win the race.

"We'll pass the bale to port, Hughie," Jerry called out. "Looks like we've got it made!"

Quickly, Hughie glanced over her shoulder. Her brothers were doing a good job with the little home-made iceboat, she decided, for it was just one length behind them and a little nearer the shore, aiming to pass the bale on the right.

She looked ahead again. Both men were standing on the shore to watch the finish, and so was Barney. Then Cass started walking out toward the straw bale, and Hughie saw Barney run after him. The dog caught and bit Cass's left boot. As before, Cass kicked out at the dog in anger; Hughie was sure he was swearing again.

Without thinking what might happen, Hughie cried out, "Barney!"

The dog heard her and immediately began running out toward *Skimmer*, now only twenty-five feet from the straw bale.

"Barney! Out of the way!" Hughie yelled. But Barney kept coming. Jerry, at the rudder, swerved sharply to miss the dog, and *Skimmer* tipped over. As Hughie let go of the lines to fall clear of the boat, she saw *Flash* cross the finish line.

"We win!" yelled Marty. He and Jim swerved after they passed the bale and came to a stop a few feet from the shore. Jerry and Hughie had *Skimmer* upright again, and no damage seemed to have been done to the pretty little iceboat. But Hughie was downcast as they pulled *Skimmer* past the straw bale, Barney following. The dog seemed to sense he had done something wrong, and his tail was "at half mast," as Jim called it.

Mr. Owens said, "A great race, all of you! I guess we'll have to call *Flash* the winner, although I'd say *Skimmer* was running a sure course to cross the line first until the dog ran out there. Seems to me you all should feel proud of the way you handled this race."

"Thank you, Mr. Owens," Jim said.

"Jerry, I'm glad you put watching out for the dog ahead of winning," Mr. Owens said. He held out his hand to Jerry, who took it and smiled as man and boy shook hands.

"We'll have a rematch when we can, Mr. Owens. But I think we'll tie Barney up next time."

Cass was standing nearby. Hughie thought he looked even uglier than last year, especially now when he was angry.

"Ought to get rid of that animal," Cass said. "He's vicious."

Jim, Marty, and Hughie all spoke together. "No, he's not!"

Marty added, "Barney never bit anybody—not even me when I was little and kept pulling his tail."

"Huh! Two times, now, he's gone after me. Don't tell me he ain't vicious!" Cass muttered a few more words about what he'd do if Barney ever attacked him again.

Mr. Owens said, "Watch your language, Cass! I've never had any trouble with Barney for the three winters we've been cutting ice here. Just leave the dog alone."

All this time, Hughie had been standing with her hand on Barney's collar. She was trying to keep from crying. If she hadn't called out Barney's name when she did, the dog wouldn't have run out at the wrong time. They'd have won the race for sure. Jerry must be really mad at her now.

Jerry said, "Well, I'd better take *Skimmer* on home. Better luck next time, Hughie."

"Maybe you'd better get someone else to crew for you, Jerry," she said, and turned her head away so that he wouldn't see the tears that came. "Come on, Barney," she said and started to walk toward the house, keeping her head down and making a quick pass at her eyes with her free mittened hand.

Jerry had turned back. "Hey, Hughie!" he called, "I don't know where I'd find a better crew! It wasn't your fault we didn't win."

Hughie still couldn't look back. In as steady a voice as she could muster she called, "Thanks, Jerry. See you later," and headed for the outhouse.

In a few minutes Hughie had herself under control again and came out of the outhouse. Barney was waiting for her, and greeted her with a wagging tail and a look of "I'm sorry I did something wrong" in his huge brown eyes.

"Oh, Barney, it's all right. You didn't mean to upset the race," she said. She looked over toward the lake. The bale of straw was gone, and Cass and Mr. Owens had both disappeared. Jerry had also left. Marty and Jim were taking the sail off their boat, preparing it for storage.

"Hey, Hughie! You all right?" Jim called to her.
"Yeah, I'm all right."

"You don't look it. You didn't hurt yourself when the boat tipped, did you?"

Hughie tried to smile. "Just my feelings, I guess."

"Hey, you couldn't help what happened. And it was just a race for fun, anyway. Cheer up."

But Hughie had more on her mind than the disappointing race. She hadn't had any luck trying to find her locket, and tomorrow the ice crew would be scraping snow off this whole part of Lake Monona. Maybe her locket would end up inside a cake of ice away off in Chicago! This was her last chance to hunt for it. "I'm going to walk a little before I go in," she said. "Come on, Barney."

Her head down, she walked out onto the ice. "Barney, I wish you could find my locket for me," she said. Barney rubbed against her right side, and she put her hand on his big head as they walked slowly along, out to where the bale of straw had been. She stopped now and then and pushed snow aside with her overshoe, thinking she might have seen a bit of metal. Only bits of straw. . . .

Hughie shivered and pulled her coat around her body. Even with her woolen clothes and heavy coat, she was becoming chilled through. What was the use of looking any more?

It had been a clear, cold day, but now the sun was dropping fast in the sky across the lake and the temperature was falling even faster. As she looked westward, Hughie saw Jerry come out onto the lake and begin the walk back to the icehouse. He waved to her, but she didn't wave back. He might want to talk about the race and she was afraid she'd start crying again.

Pretending not to have seen him, she turned and went ashore, Barney at her heels. She felt very tired.

CHAPTER *9

Tuesday was back-to-school day for four Rileys, and chores had to be done quickly. After her mother woke her, Hughie's first job was to rouse her sister Nora, youngest of the four to go to school. Feeding Barney was her last job. While she was eating, Hughie got a length of clothesline from the cowshed. She slipped one end through a metal ring on the dog's collar, tied it firmly, and looped the other end around a tree.

"Hate to do this to you, Barn, but you've got to stay clear of the workmen." Barney's eyes looked sadder than usual as he paused in his eating to look at her.

At eight o'clock the four left for school. It was a walk of more than two miles. Papa insisted that the boys walk with their sisters. If one was tardy they all would be. In the snow, Nora couldn't walk fast enough for them to get to school on time, so Marty and Jim pulled a sled on which Nora rode, along with the boys' schoolbooks. Hughie carried the dinner pail, with lunch for all four of them, and her own books.

When Jim grumbled about having to walk with girls, Hughie just grunted. "You think it's tough for you. How do you think I like having to walk with all you little kids? And how would you feel if you'd had to wait to start first grade until your little brother was old enough to tag along?"

Papa hadn't wanted Hughie to walk that far alone, and she had never forgotten how awful it was to be eight years old and in first grade along with Jim and two other six-year-olds. Fortunately, Papa had already taught her to read, using the newspaper for lessons, so she had moved up to the third grade quite soon. Now she was in the seventh, along with Mary Schultz, Tim Tompkins, another boy, and a seatmate in a double-wide desk, Edna Hofmeister.

The bell in the little cupola tower on top of the school was ringing as the Rileys reached the schoolyard. Jim took the sled around to the side of the building as the others headed for the door leading to the entry hall. A hook was there for each child's coat, and overshoes and lunch buckets were put on the floor. The teacher, Miss Fenton, a shawl pulled around her shoulders, stood in the doorway leading to the single classroom.

"Keep your coats on for a while, boys and girls," she said. "The school got terribly cold over the holidays, but we'll soon have it warm enough."

Nora sat with the other children in the primary grades at desks off to the left. Jim and Mary's class rows came next, and the sixth-, seventh-, and eighth-graders sat near the right-hand wall. As Hughie went to her desk, she glanced at the eighth-grade section to see if Jerry was there. He was, but Julie Schultz was absent.

A large heating stove on a square fireproof base sat in the center of the room, its smokepipe going up through the ceiling and over to the chimney. Miss Fenton had arrived an hour before the children and had a good fire burning, but cold air still lingered around the room's edges and the windows were swirled with frost ferns.

She rang the little brass bell that was always on her desk, and the children were immediately quiet. "I trust you all had happy holidays and are ready to start this brand new year—and century—by doing your very best work. For now, all stand. We shall salute the flag and recite the Pledge of Allegiance."

And so the day started. Study assignments were made, and one class after another was called to the front of the room for recitation.

Hughie had a page of arithmetic problems to solve. She worked each one on her slate before copying it on paper. One was a great long column of six-digit numbers to be added. When she finished adding, she added it again to check her total, but came up with a different figure.

She sighed. Looking to the front of the room, she saw that Marty's class had been called up to read. The selection from McGuffey's *Fourth Eclectic Reader* was "The Old Slate."

One of the little girls was asked to start the story aloud. She read, " 'I have a great mind to break this stupid old slate,' said little Willie, one morning, as he sat over his first example in subtraction."

"Very good, Della," said Miss Fenton. "Martin Riley, next sentence."

" 'Why, what has the poor slate done?' asked the pleasant voice of his sister Grace, behind him." As Marty finished, he looked up and made a face at Hughie, who suppressed a giggle.

She let herself listen to the story of little Willie, who

wanted to break his slate because it wouldn't do his arithmetic for him and who blamed everyone but himself for not having his homework finished. Hughie turned back to her own slate, on which she had changed the total three times already. *Yeah. You dumb old slate! You keep giving me wrong answers! Wish I could change you into one of those adding machines like they have at the bank. When I get married, I'll never have to add up stuff like this, anyway.* She looked at her seatmate's neat page of carefully copied arithmetic problems.

"What did you get for number seven, Edna?" she whispered, and leaned over to compare her answer.

"Ellen Riley, are you copying a sum?" Miss Fenton was suddenly right beside Hughie.

Hughie sighed. "No, ma'am. I just wanted to see if I had the same answer."

"Well, I hope that's *all* you were doing. Just add it again to find out if it's right." Miss Fenton raised her voice. "Fifth grade to the front for geography."

Jim's class, which had only three members, was soon naming the forty-five states of the Union and the capital city of each one. Hughie knew she'd better keep her mind on her own work or she'd have extra homework— and there'd be enough to do helping Mama tonight as it was. She finally decided on the sum of the long problem and copied it neatly on paper.

Then her mind drifted again, this time to what the ice crew would be doing. They'd have the snowplows out on the lake. Would her locket have been uncovered? As soon as she got home, she'd look along the snow-piles they'd have scraped up. Maybe—

Miss Fenton's voice interrupted her thoughts. "Boys and girls, it's twelve o'clock."

It was lunchtime at last. All the Riley children's lunches were in the covered tin molasses pail that Hughie filled each morning. This cold day the children had to eat in the schoolroom. By noon it was finally warm enough to take off their coats, but it still was much warmer near the stove than over near the walls.

As one of the eighth-grade boys, Jerry shared the duty of keeping the fire going in the stove. He threw in another chunk of wood and said, "Hey, Rileys, bring your lunch over here nearer the stove!"

He had placed his dinner pail on the nearest desktop, and Jim and Marty hurried over. Jerry shared with his little sister, Genevieve, who was in the third grade with Nora. The two little girls sat together to eat lunch. Hughie got the Riley lunch pail from the cloakroom and perched on the low desk the girls shared, facing the boys. Soon she had passed around the sandwiches, apples, and cookies.

When they'd all started eating, Marty said, "Jerry, I'll bet you're mad at Hughie for making you lose the race. That was a dumb thing she did."

Jerry looked at Hughie, who chose to concentrate on her jelly sandwich. "I wouldn't say it was dumb, Marty. She didn't want old Barney to get any more kicks from that guy Cass. I don't blame her. And we'll beat you next time we race, you just wait and see!"

"Huh!" said Jim. "Won't get a chance till time for the ice to start melting, 'less we go way down to the other end where they aren't cutting."

"Well, that's what we'll do, won't we, Hughie?"

"Sure, Jerry." Hughie could look up now and smile; Jerry still wanted her for crew. Thinking of the race reminded her of Mr. Cass, and she added, "I wish you had one of the other men for boss. That Cass gives me the creeps."

"Me too," Jerry said. "But he goes with the job, and I want to earn a little money on my own. I don't like to ask my father for money for some things, like the Valentine's Day party. Julie wants me to take her."

Hughie was glad it was time to close up the lunch pail and go back to her seat for the afternoon classes. *Guess I'm still just like a brother to him—good enough for crew, but not to take to a party.*

When school ended for the day, Jerry walked home with the Rileys, helping to pull the sled, which Nora now shared with Genevieve. The little girls had an exciting ride, for the boys walked extra fast and even ran part of the way. Jerry set the pace, as he was anxious to get home, change to clothes he could wear in the stable, and begin his job.

Hughie kept up with them. Since they were all home early, she decided she could take time to go out to the edge of the ice for a few minutes before she went inside to help her mother. Nora went into the house, but Hughie, Jim, and Marty hurried around to the lakeshore to see what was going on.

Barney came out of his doghouse as soon as he heard the children. When the rope stopped him short, he barked his complaint.

"Oh, poor old Barney," Hughie said as she stopped to pet him for a moment. "But you know why you're tied, don't you? It'll keep you away from that mean old Cass.''

She followed the boys over the railroad track to the edge of frozen Lake Monona. The men were still clearing snow from the area where ice was to be cut, a huge square about six hundred feet on each side. It reached almost up to the Byrnes place and far out onto the lake. There were six ice planes out there. These were wide sleds, each with a tilted blade under it to push the snow away, drawn by a sturdy workhorse. A man sat on each sled, to guide the horse and add his own weight to the plane. The ice planes were working the surface carefully, each one overlapping the area partially cleared by the one ahead of it.

A huge snow bank was already built up off to Hughie's left as she stood watching. She walked as close to it as she dared without getting in the way of the workers, more of whom had arrived during the day. She scanned the pile but saw no shining bit of metal.

Maybe it's still out there, she thought. Wish I dared go out and look. A plane had already scraped the area once where she and Jim had been rolling around that day, and another was approaching it. She saw Cass directing the work out there. He'd shout at her if she went near.

Just as Jerry arrived and was running out to report to Cass, Mama called, ''Hughie! Come in, please!'' Reluctantly, she turned and went inside.

Her first duty was to change from her school clothes to an old dress, so she went quickly to her bedroom. As she came back to the kitchen, she said. ''Oh, those pies smell good, Mama!''

Minnie, the helper from last year, had arrived that morning to begin work. She and Mrs. Riley had baked four apple pies and were taking them from the oven. Cinnamony juice still bubbled from slits in the golden crusts. On a plate were some rolls made from the scraps of leftover pie crust dough.

Mrs. Riley said, "Help yourself to the crust rolls—but not to any pie, honey. I think we have enough for the family to have some for supper, unless the other ten men show up before then. I certainly hope they don't. Minnie and I are figuring on just feeding ten this evening."

The next hour passed quickly. Mrs. Riley had several small tasks for Hughie and then put her to work peeling potatoes. The men would eat two huge bowls of mashed potatoes, besides what the eight Rileys would want. Minnie sat down at the table and helped with the peeling, and finally there were enough potatoes ready to be boiled.

As Hughie was drying her hands, her mother said, "Go into the dining room, dear, and get out knives, forks, and plates. Better set twelve places, just in case I missed counting a couple of men."

"Yes, Mama." Nora, Beth, and Rose were playing with dolls off to one side of the kitchen range, out of the way, and Hughie glanced at them enviously. Wish I wasn't the oldest one and could just play like that, she thought, as she had so many times before.

When the places were set, she reported back to her mother. "What now, Mama?"

"Put your coat back on and go to the cellar for me. I

need two jars of pickled peaches and one of apple butter. Then fill up the basket with apples, please."

Hughie sighed again. How she hated going to the cellar alone, especially when darkness was coming! But she knew Mama was getting very tired, and she'd better not complain. She said, "Okay, Mama," and went out to the chilly storeroom, put on her coat, and took the basket from its hook on the wall.

She shivered, when she stepped out onto the porch, and pulled her coat closer. As she went down the porch steps she saw lantern light shining from the window of the stable section of the icehouse. Jerry would be feeding the horses now, she decided. Then the light broadened as the door opened and the silhouette of a man darkened the doorway.

"I'd better hurry. The men will be coming in to supper," she said aloud, and went around to the side of the house where the cellar entrance was.

With the heavy door pulled up, she went down the steps, pushed open the door, and felt for the candle and matches. When the candle was lighted she pushed the door closed behind her to keep out the cold. Then, holding the candle, she checked the shelves until she found the pickled peaches and put two jars into the basket.

"Now for the apple butter." Her voice sounded strangely hollow in the stone-walled room. When she had found the apple butter, she put a jar into the basket and set the candle on a shelf. Then she turned to the apple barrel and reached in.

She had the basket almost full of apples and was leaning over to get just a few more when she heard a sound. She straightened up quickly. The sound she heard couldn't have been just mice scurrying. Someone was coming down the steps to the cellar.

She turned quickly as the door opened and a man entered. "Now, missy, I have something to tell you," said Cass.

He pushed the door closed behind him.

CHAPTER * 10

Hughie felt a sudden prickling on her face and a sinking feeling inside. She stooped to set the basket down on the hard-packed dirt of the cellar floor. As she stood up again, she swallowed hard and took a deep breath to calm herself. Her voice was almost normal as she spoke.

"I've got to take this basket up to the kitchen, Mr. Cass. So if you have something to tell me, please do it quickly."

"Come on now, missy. You should be glad to take a few minutes to be friendly with old Cass."

He stepped toward her. Hughie backed away.

"I'm not going to hurt you, missy. I just want you to be nice to me for a minute. You've grown real purty, I think." He reached out and put a finger under Hughie's chin.

She turned her head, trying to pull away. She could go back no farther, for the shelf edges were against her shoulder blades. Cass was so close that she could smell his chewing tobacco and see the red-brown stain of it on his droopy mustache. Pushing his hand away, she tried to step around him toward the door, but he grasped her arms just below the shoulders. The glint in his pale blue eyes made her even more fearful.

Trying to sound calm, she said, "What did you want to tell me? My mother needs these things for supper."

"Ain't no hurry. The gang ain't all inside yet. What I want to tell you is that I've got somethin' you want."

"What?"

"I ain't gonna tell you till you're nice to me. Gimme a little kiss, honey."

He pushed his bristly face against her cheek and pulled her close to him.

"No!" Hughie pushed against Cass's chest with her hands, but it did no good. His grasp tightened.

"Don't be like that, missy! Just give me one little sweet kiss, and I'll tell you what I've got in my pocket."

"No!" An empty canning jar fell from the shelf as Hughie tried to pull away. She could feel that wet mustache as Cass pressed his lips to her mouth. Hughie turned her head from side to side to escape, but Cass persisted.

"Don't—" she tried to say, but it was muffled. Then, to her surprise, Cass backed off.

"That's no way to be nice to me. Kissin' ain't no fun like that. And you look like such a sweet thing, with them nice blue eyes and that red-brown hair!" Cass put his hand into his right-hand coat pocket. "Right here, in my hand, I have something' real nice that you want. You want it real bad, I think. Seen you out there lookin' for somethin', and I've got it right here."

Her locket! Cass must have her locket!

"Give it to me and then I'll let you kiss me," she forced herself to say.

"Oh, no! The kiss comes first." Cass was pressing himself against her now, his coat flung open. He un-buttoned her coat, too, and put his arms around her waist, forcing her body toward his.

There was a thudding sound of someone coming fast down the cellar steps. Cass backed away from Hughie as the doorknob was turned, and Hughie quickly wiped her mouth with her coat sleeve.

"Hughie! Mama said to get back upstairs. She needs that stuff!" Jim stood there, a look of surprise on his face as he saw Cass, who was bending over to pick up the basket.

"What're you doin' here?" Jim asked.

"Thought the little miss would need help carryin' all this stuff," Cass said. He walked toward the door with the full basket.

"I'll take it," Jim said. "Hughie doesn't need your help."

"Okay, okay. Don't get huffy, kid," Cass said, handing the basket to Jim. He left the cellar and clumped up the steps.

Jim turned to Hughie. "What was he really doin' down here, Hughie?"

Hughie busied herself putting out the candle and setting it in its place. "I'm glad you came, Jim. I'm afraid of him."

As they went up the steps, Jim asked, "What did he do? Was he tryin' to kiss you or somethin'?"

Hughie was afraid to say too much. "Kinda, I guess," she said and hurried toward the back porch.

"I'll tell Papa and he'll fix him!" Jim said. He lowered the cellar door, picked up the basket again, and hurried after Hughie.

"No! Don't tell Papa, Jim. Promise me!" She turned toward him, a pleading look in her eyes.

"Why shouldn't I tell Papa? You want that Cass gettin' mushy over you? Thought you didn't like him."

"I don't. And I'll watch out that he doesn't follow me down there again."

"But why shouldn't I tell Papa? Then you wouldn't have to worry about it. He'd tell Mr. Owens and Owens would fire Cass—just like that!"

Hughie knew she'd have to tell Jim more. "He—he found something of mine, Jim. If Papa gets after him I might not get it back." Cass would have known the locket was hers just by opening it and seeing the picture Grandma had put into it.

"I still think I ought to tell Papa. What did he find that's so important, anyway?"

Hughie paused before answering Jim's insistent question. They were on the back porch when she said, "It's kind of a secret, Jim, but something I need. Please don't say anything. I'll get what he found back, and then I'll tell Papa if he bothers me any more. Please, Jim— promise you won't tell."

Jim was reaching for the doorknob. "Well, it seems kinda funny you don't want me to tell on Cass, but I won't say anything if you don't want me to. But if I catch him botherin' you again, the promise is off."

They entered the storeroom. Hughie said, "Thanks, Jim. I'll do something for you sometime. Don't say a word about it to Mama either."

Coats hung up, they entered the kitchen. Mama looked up quickly. "What took you so long, Hughie?"

"I'm sorry, Mama. Couldn't find all the stuff, I guess." Hughie busied herself opening a jar of pickled peaches. She didn't let Mama get a good look at her—

somehow, Mama always knew when something was wrong.

Mrs. Riley was too busy to notice anything unusual. "The rest of the workmen just got here, and we're trying to fix enough to feed them. Hughie, go in and set eight more places."

There were now the twenty men of the ice crew to serve, besides Mr. Owens. Hughie got out eight more plates, knives, and forks, adding four to each side of the table. As she worked, she thought about the unpleasant encounter with Cass. How could she get her locket without "being nice" to him? She shuddered at the thought. Somehow, she'd have to get him to give it to her—or maybe she could find a way to reach into his coat pocket and take it. She wondered where he hung the coat when he took it off. . . .

She looked up quickly as she heard a man enter the room, fearful that it might be Cass. With relief, she saw that it was Lars Olson, one of the men she remembered from the year before as always cheerful. He was a sailor on the Great Lakes in the warmer months and spent the ice-bound winters working for the Knickerbocker Ice Company. He took off his dark blue knitted cap as he greeted her.

"Hello, Mr. Olson," Hughie said. "I'm real glad to see you."

I sure am! she thought as she hurried back to the kitchen. Papa was home, and she'd have to get the family table ready, help with the baby, and do all sorts of things that Mama didn't have time to do when there were so many men to feed. There was no time now to wonder what to do about Cass.

*   *   *

The next day at school, Hughie kept hoping for a chance to speak to Jerry when no one else could hear. Maybe he'd seen Cass pick up her locket. He might even try to get it out of Cass's coat pocket for her. But Julie was back, and when the noon hour came she leaned on Jerry's arm and limped over to where they were all about to eat lunch.

"How's your ankle now, Julie?" Hughie asked.

Julie thrust her foot forward and pulled her skirt up a bit. "You can see it's still terribly sore and swollen. I can hardly bear to walk on it!" Her voice sounded much weaker than usual.

Hughie looked down at Julie's fine black kid shoe. It was laced high, but the shoelaces were allowed to be very loose over the ankle, which didn't look a bit swollen to Hughie.

Julie immediately turned her attention to Jerry. "Oh, Jerry! I forgot to bring my lunch pail from the cloak-room. Get it for me."

Jerry, who was already opening his own lunch bucket, said, " 'Please get it for me, Jerry.' "

Julie pouted a bit. "Oh, Jerry, don't be mean! Get it for me please, Jerry."

He grinned. "That's better. But I'll be glad when that ankle mends so you can wait on yourself."

As he left, Hughie said, "You really ought to pull the laces tighter to get your ankle better, Julie. Dr. Byrnes said a tight binding was best."

"Oh, no, that would hurt more. He didn't say that at all."

"Suit yourself," Hughie said. She poured milk into four tin cups and divided up the sandwiches for the boys, Nora, and herself.

A few minutes later, when they were all eating, Julie wrinkled up her nose. "It smells like a stable in here."

Jerry looked quickly at the soles of his shoes. " 'Scuse me a minute," he said, and walked to the front entry. When he came back, he said, "I thought I had cleaned my shoes, but I guess there was still some stable muck on the soles. Sorry."

Julie sniffed again. "I should think you would be. That stinky stuff! I don't know why you have to do something as vulgar as cleaning a stable anyway."

"Because there aren't many ways a kid can earn money around here."

"Your father would give you money, wouldn't he?"

"Sure, but a guy likes to feel he's on his own a little— at least for money to pay for special things."

Julie shrugged her shoulders. "Well, I suppose it's all right—if it's for things like buying me candy or flowers. But I do think you could do something not so smelly."

She's awfully sure the candy and flowers will be for her! Hughie thought. But she's probably right. She began collecting the lunch wrappings and tin cups to put back into the bucket.

Jerry said, "I won't be so stinky after this. My mother said I had to get home early enough to take off *all* my school clothes and put on my old jeans and boots before I go to work. I didn't have time yesterday, so I wore my school shoes when I cleaned the stable. Starting today, I have to go home fifteen minutes before the rest of you."

"You lucky dog!" said Jim. "Sure wish I had that job."

"You might not like it when your arms ached so

much you couldn't get to sleep. Lifting a loaded pitchfork isn't easy," Jerry said. "But maybe next year you'll have a chance at it. I'll be in high school then, and I might be able to get a job delivering groceries after school."

Miss Fenton rang her bell to signal it was time for afternoon classes to begin, and Jerry helped Julie limp back to her seat, in front of his own. Hughie still hadn't had a chance to speak to him alone.

When school was out, after Jerry had left, Hughie noticed that Julie tightened the laces around her injured ankle and managed to walk off with scarcely a sign of a limp.

If Jerry were here, she'd be helpless again! She couldn't help but think Julie was just working on Jerry's sympathies. And he seemed to like it. Well, if that was what it took to get a boy to pay attention to her, she guessed she'd grow up to be an old maid schoolteacher, like Miss Fenton.

CHAPTER * 11

Back home after school, Hughie walked to the lake with Jim and Marty to see how the work was coming along. The whole big square had been cleared of snow, and now there were white snow hills on three sides. Special horse-drawn sleds were on the ice, starting the job of cutting.

"Gee, what are they doing now?" Marty asked. He'd been too young to learn much about ice harvesting the year before.

Jim explained, from his superior vantage point. "First they mark off a big square, real straight. Now see that guy riding on a sort of sled over there on the far side? He's following the straight line very carefully."

"Yeah," Marty said. "I remember now. He calls that sled a snow plane, and it's got blades to cut lines for the other cutters to follow."

A horse was moving slowly along, pulling the snow plane. Just behind him was another horse-drawn sled, and a little nearer to the watching children came still another one.

"I guess some big pieces will be cut off pretty soon," Jim said.

Hughie shook her head. "Uh-unh, not yet, Jim. That ice out there is at least eighteen inches thick. They have to cut it a little at a time, deeper and deeper each trip over the ice. Last year Mr. Owens told me the lines have to be exactly forty-four inches apart. They keep one blade in the line that the plane ahead of them cut."

They watched for a while longer as the horse-drawn sleds followed one after another. Away off other cutters were starting to crisscross the first grooves with cuts six feet apart, marking off rectangles. The final size of the ice slabs would be six feet long by forty-four inches wide.

"Let's see," Hughie said. "This is Wednesday. I'll bet they get the first big block of ice out on Saturday."

"That would be great—we'd be home from school to see it," Marty said.

Jim took hold of his brother's sleeve. "Come on, Marty, let's go out on the ice so we can see better."

As the boys walked away, Hughie heard Barney whimper. His rope was stretched as far as it could go. His tail wagged slowly and his big eyes pleaded for attention. Hughie glanced over her shoulder to see if Cass was around, but he was not in sight. She walked over to the dog.

"Poor Barney!" she said. "Do you want to run a little?"

Barney's tail wagged faster, and he wiggled all over as Hughie untied the rope. But as soon as he was loose he bounded out toward Jim and Marty.

"No, Barney, not that way!" Hughie called out.

Barney pretended not to hear and ran out onto the ice.

"Barney! Come back here!" Hughie yelled.

Just then Jerry arrived for work. He ran right past

Hughie and in a moment was out on the ice and had hold of Barney's collar.

"I've got him!" he called. He stopped for a moment to pat Barney's head and quiet him. "Barney, you'd better not run out here like that. You could go right over the edge when they take out the ice! Now let's go back." Jerry kept a grip on the dog's collar as they walked toward Hughie, who had come partway to meet them.

"Thanks, Jerry," she said as she took charge of the dog. "I know you've got to get to work, but I want to ask you something."

"Okay, Hughie. But I don't want Cass to see me standing here, so make it fast."

"I think Cass found my locket. Did you see him pick up anything from the ice?"

Jerry thought back. "Yeah, I was going out to lead in a horse and I saw him looking at something he'd picked up. It could have been your locket."

"Now I *know* he's got it!" Hughie said.

"Hey, I gotta go. Cass'll be out yelling at me."

"Well, thanks anyway, Jerry. Tell you more later."

Jerry headed for the icehouse as Hughie took Barney back.

"Cheer up, Barney," she said as she tied the rope with a double knot. "I know how you feel, but the ice crew won't be here forever. We'll both be glad when they go, won't we?"

As she headed for the house, a hopeful thought came to her. Cass didn't wear his coat when he ate. Could she slip up to the dormitory without anyone knowing and find it? She thought about how she might do this as she changed from her school clothes and came back to the kitchen. Mama and Minnie were putting the top crusts onto six dried peach pies, and the room was warm from the hot range.

"I'm ready to help, Mama," she said.

As she checked the temperature in the oven, Mrs. Riley said, "One thing Minnie and I haven't had time for, Hughie, is to refill the water pitchers in the dormitory."

Maybe my locket's up there now and I can find it, Hughie thought as she pumped rainwater from the cistern pump at the sink. She carefully carried the bucket of water, with a dipper in it, up the stairs. Along the dormitory wall at the top of the stairway were four washstands that the men shared, with water pitchers and washbasins on them. She divided the bucket of water among the pitchers.

There were hooks on the wall between the washstands where the men could hang their coats and other clothing. Hughie wondered which hook Cass would use. Each man had a small trunk, with his name or initials stenciled on it, at the foot of his cot. I'll look at the trunks and see which one is his, she decided. He'd probably use the hook across from it.

C. Cass was on the third trunk from the left end as she faced the cots. His hook would be right near the top of the stairway, and it would be easy to check the coat pockets quickly.

I'll come up while the men are eating, she planned. That was the only time the coat would be there with no men present. And then she realized that Cass would probably see her opening the stairway door. He might even leave the table and follow her. She sighed. That plan wouldn't work.

Between the cots were nightstands, each with two drawers. Maybe he put the locket in his drawer! Hastily, she opened and quickly searched the drawers in the nightstand Cass would use. The only gold object she saw was the button he used to hold his stiff collar to his shirt when he dressed up. She raised the lid of Cass's trunk and rummaged hastily through the tray. No locket and chain. He must still have it with him, she decided. How could she get it?

Discouraged, she picked up the empty bucket and its dipper and went downstairs. Minnie was alone in the kitchen, peeling potatoes. "Took you long enough," she complained. "Your ma's gone out to milk Bessie. She said to tell you to bring the baby out here and give her some milk and a graham cracker."

As she lifted Rose from her crib, Hughie sighed deeply, her mind on her problems. Why had she worn the locket when she wasn't supposed to, anyway? She wouldn't be having all this trouble if she'd obeyed her mother to start with.

If only she could figure out some way to get it back without having to be alone with Cass! She was really afraid of having Cass find her alone in the dining room. Hughie decided to ask Mama if Nora could help her set and clear tables.

Mrs. Riley agreed that Nora was old enough to help, and the two girls started working together that evening.

Until suppertime Friday, Hughie had no contact with Cass. The workers had just finished eating when the two girls went into the dining room to start taking their dishes to the kitchen so that Minnie could wash them. Only a few men were still sitting at the table, talking and finishing their coffee.

Hughie saw that Cass was among them and was careful not to meet his eyes. As she fixed a small stack of dishes for Nora to carry to the kitchen, she sensed that Cass was watching her. She gathered more plates, cups, knives, and forks and was about to go to the kitchen with them when Cass rose from his place.

"Miss, just a minute," he said. Hughie stopped. Two of the other men were watching, so she tried to act as if this were nothing more than a request for some change in the service.

Cass came so close she could feel his breath on her cheek, but he didn't touch her. He said, in a voice so low that only she could hear, "Don't forget our little talk. You don't have school tomorrow, so come out to the stable after dinner—and don't bring your brother."

Without answering, Hughie went to the kitchen with the stack of dishes. As she set them down next to where Minnie had the dishpan on the oilcloth-covered table, the cups slipped off the stack.

Minnie caught them before they fell to the floor and looked sharply at Hughie. "Well, land sakes, girl, what's the matter with you? You look like you seen a ghost!"

Hughie pulled her mind back to the kitchen. "Uh—sorry, Minnie, I guess I wasn't paying attention to what I was doing."

"You all right, girl? You sick or somep'n? You been awful quiet the last couple days."

Hughie made an effort to look more cheerful. "I'm all

right, Minnie. Guess I'm kinda tired from all the extra work this week."

"Well, you ain't the only one! Your ma hardly ever has a minute to sit down, and I'm 'bout to drop in my tracks when I get home nights. Get on in there and bring the rest o' them dishes so's I kin get through here."

Cass was gone, as were the other men, when Hughie returned to the dining room. Nora was there ahead of her, with more dishes stacked. The two of them cleared the table with one more trip.

"You're a big help, Nora," Hughie said. "Thanks."

Most evenings, homework lasted until bedtime after the evening chores were done, but Fridays were special. Homework could wait until later in the weekend. Papa read aloud from the newspaper as they sat around the table in the kitchen until Mama announced, "Bedtime for three little girls!"

By half past eight, the baby was asleep and Nora and Beth were huddled together in the bed they shared with Hughie, trying to get warm enough for sleeping. Marty, Jim, and Hughie were playing Old Maid at one end of the table.

Hughie's mind wasn't on the card game. Usually, she was the winner, but this evening she was left with the Old Maid card two times in a row.

"Hey, Hughie, your head's in the clouds," Jim said. "She just threw that game away, didn't she, Mart?"

"I guess I'm too tired to think any more tonight," Hughie said. "You two play without me."

"Getting too late for another game, boys," their mother said. "Off to bed for you both."

As Jim and Marty left after only feeble protests, Hughie moved around to sit next to her father at the end of the table. He had finished reading the paper. Mama had taken out her mending basket, but she set down the sock she'd been darning.

"It's good to just sit and do nothing for a change," she said. "I think I'll go to bed soon myself. Tomorrow is Saturday, but I have to be up early. I promised the men hot biscuits for breakfast."

Mr. Riley folded the newspaper and looked at his wife and Hughie. "Both of you look worn out," he remarked. "My, but it will be good when the last of the crew leaves and we can be a family again!"

There was only the sound of the clock on the shelf above the sink ticking the seconds away. Then Mr. Riley stood up and stretched. "Three weeks from now the icehouse will be filled and we can all get back to normal. In the meantime, I think we'd better get some sleep. Morning'll be here before we know it."

Mrs. Riley said, "You go ahead, James. I want to talk with Hughie a few minutes." When he had gone into the bedroom, she said, "I think something besides the work is bothering you, Hughie."

Hughie looked up quickly. Did her worries show that much? She had a sinking feeling that Mama knew what was wrong and was going to ask about the locket. She was trying to get up the courage to say she had lost it when Mrs. Riley spoke again, and the need to explain was gone. Hughie felt relieved.

"Are you feeling sick and just not saying anything, dear?"

Hughie forced herself to smile. "No, Mama. Just

tired. School's kind of hard in seventh grade, and there's so much I have to do here too." She paused. Then she said, "Lots of times I wish I wasn't the oldest."

"Well, dear, I really don't know how I'd manage without you."

Hughie reached out and touched her mother's hand. "I love you, Mama."

"I know you do, honey, and your father and I both love you a great deal. We are very proud of our oldest daughter. And Hughie, there are good things that go with being the oldest, too."

"Like what?"

Her mother laughed. "Like getting first chance at the bath water, for one. Like staying up a little later than the others, for another."

"And being named after you and Grandmother."

"And that reminds me of something extra special that's for you just *because* you're the oldest," her mother said.

"What, Mama?"

"You have to promise to keep it a secret for a while."

"Cross my heart, Mama. Tell me!"

"A letter came from your grandma today. Aunt Effie is much better, and Grandma sent her love to all of us."

"Is that the secret?" Hughie's voice showed disappointment.

"No, of course not. Grandma has a surprise just for you. I really shouldn't tell you—"

"Oh, Mama! Please! I won't tell anybody else. Please tell me!"

"Well, all right. When your birthday comes in May,

and school is out, Grandma wants you to go to Chicago to visit her."

Hughie was entranced. "Oh, I'll get to ride on the train! And see the boats on Lake Michigan that Mr. Olson talks about, and the big stores, and—"

"And the museums and lots of other things, Grandma says. She wrote that she'll even take you to dinner at a big hotel."

Hughie got up and hugged her mother. "Oh, Mama, I can hardly wait! I'm glad now that I *am* the oldest!"

"But remember, Hughie, you're to keep it a secret. Grandma wants the fun of telling you herself when she comes to visit us in March."

"She's coming here in March?"

"Yes, dear. That's another nice surprise. Now let's get to bed."

Mrs. Riley was lowering the wick in the hanging lamp and didn't see the sudden change in her daughter's eyes. The happiness was gone, and in its place was worry. *What will Grandma think of me if I don't have the locket?*

CHAPTER * 12

Saturday was a cold, clear day, so bright with sparkling snow that when Hughie went outside to feed Barney she had to shield her eyes. When he heard her coming, Barney came out of his house and greeted her joyfully. For a moment, the girl's mind turned away from her worries about what the day was to bring, and she hugged the big dog, holding the bowl high.

Barney barked in protest.

"All right, here you are, Barney!" She put down the bowl of food for him. It was full, for with so many men to feed, there were lots of table scraps. "That'll fill you up," she said. Then she added, "You're a good dog. I bet you wish you could run around like you can when the men aren't here."

Barney looked up from his food for a moment as if to agree.

"Tell you what. When Mama doesn't need me to help any more, I'll come out and let you have a good run. But you'll have to promise me not to go out on the ice!"

She patted his head. The dog's tail wagged, a waving brown and white plume, and his glance seemed to say, I promise.

"Gotta go now," Hughie said as she straightened up. She walked over to where her snow fort still stood, a shapeless mound now, from the snow that had fallen on it since that day—the day she'd lost her locket.

"Hi, Hughie!" It was Jerry, coming from the road.

"Oh, hi, Jerry! Do you have to work this morning?"

"Just long enough to help get four horses ready to be sent back to Chicago on the noon freight train. They don't need as many horses now that the clearing and cutting are mostly done. Then I'll be off until I come back to clean the stable. I can do that 'most any time this afternoon."

He was about to go inside. "Jerry," Hughie said, "I think my locket is still in Cass's coat pocket. Do you think you could reach in and get it when he's not looking?"

Jerry shook his head. "No, Hughie, the only time he takes his coat off is when he's in his office, where it's warmer—and he'd be right there. The only way I could do it is if he went outside without putting it on."

Hughie decided she'd better tell him what she had to do. "He said I should come alone to the stable right after dinner today, when I'm through helping Mama and Minnie. I'm scared, Jerry, but I just gotta get that locket. My grandma gave it to me, and she's coming to visit—she'll hate me for losing it!"

Jerry's blue eyes looked troubled as he met Hughie's gaze. He reached up and pushed his stocking cap back a bit and then he said, "We'll get it back from that guy somehow. But I don't blame you for being scared. Know what?"

"What?"

"I think when you have to go in there would be a good time for me to clean the stable."

Hughie reached out a hand to his sleeve. "Oh, Jerry, would you? I'll count on your showing up before he gets too bad—but give me a few minutes to try to get the locket."

"Whatta ya mean—gets too bad?"

"That night down in the cellar he was trying to kiss me and he was pushing against me—that kinda stuff."

"Okay, Hughie." Jerry grinned. "Cheer up. I'll come in like a hero to the rescue!"

Hughie felt as if a weight had just been lifted from her shoulders. She laughed. "Just like in the old stories—the prince comes to save the damsel in distress." They were grinning widely at each other. "Do I ever feel better now!" Looking over his shoulder she saw that the stable door was opening and she could see Cass. She moved away quickly. "There's Cass now. G'by."

Jerry turned and hurried toward the stable. Hughie went back to the house and soon was busy at the jobs her mother assigned to her. One task was to go upstairs with Minnie to tidy the dormitory. While Minnie was taking down the slop jars to empty them, Hughie made another quick search of Cass's drawer and trunk tray. But again, no sign of the locket.

Hughie had a feeling of dread all morning as she worked. When the big noon meal was ready and the men trooped in from the lake, Minnie did all the serving. Then the whole family, except for Papa, who had to work on Saturdays, sat down at the kitchen table.

Mrs. Riley noticed that Hughie was not eating with her usual gusto. "Hughie, I thought you'd be feeling better today," she said. "What in the world is bothering you?"

This was definitely not the time to discuss her problems. "Nothing, Mama," she said. "I'm just not very hungry. Guess I'm kinda tired."

"Well, you've been working hard. After you help clear up the dinner dishes, Minnie and I won't need you until near suppertime. You can go outside and get some of this good sunshine."

Hughie was cheered by this news. At least she'd not have to make up some excuse for going out, and she could slip into the stable when no one was watching.

As she cleared dishes from the table, only a few men were still sitting there, relaxing before returning to work. Cass was not among them.

When the dishes were dried and put away, and Hughie had set Rose in her crib for a nap, Mrs. Riley said, "All of you, go and have fun for a while."

"Hooray!" said Marty. "Let's take the bobsled up the hill, Jim."

"Yeah! You wanna come too, Hughie?" Jim asked as he headed for the storeroom.

"After a while I'll come up there," Hughie said. "First I want to see how far the work on the ice cutting has gone."

"You were right about their starting to load the ice-house today. They have the first section out," Jim said. "See you later."

Outside, Hughie put off going in to see Cass. The thought of it made her feel sick to her stomach, even though she hadn't eaten much. She kept her promise to Barney to let him run free for a few minutes, in front of the house away from the working crew.

When he was panting, she led him back to where the rope end lay on the ground. As they walked past the path that led to the stable door, the awful sinking feeling came back worse than before. Soon she would have to open that latch and meet with Cass.

Her fingers were shaking as she pushed the rope end through the metal ring on Barney's collar, and her mind was not on her task as she tied the knot. "Wish you could go with me, Barney," she said. "You'd take care of that guy for me, wouldn't you?" As she turned away, she decided Barney's low whimper meant agreement.

To delay the moment of facing Cass a little longer, she went to the lakeshore to see how the ice cutting was progressing. Looking out at the ice field, now all marked off in rectangles, she thought it looked like a great sheet cake, cut and ready for serving—except that one large piece, quite close to shore, had already been taken out, exposing the black water beneath it. Men stood at the edges of another section about twenty-four feet square, working with long-handled chisels and handsaws to break that section loose. As she watched, the men separated it from the "cake" and floated it like a raft to a loading ramp near the other end of the icehouse.

To her right along the icehouse wall, she saw that the scaffolding was in place about four feet off the ground. Icehouse filling had begun. On the scaffold, a moving belt, about four feet wide, carried a slab of ice to where men waited at an opening to push it inside.

Hughie could hear the hissing of the steam engine

that powered the belt, at the west end of the icehouse. She looked down that way and saw workers standing on the floating ice cake they'd just set free, using their saws and chisels to break off one of the six-foot slabs. Men on shore reached out with prods to pull it toward them and then hoisted the heavy chunk of ice onto the moving belt. Fascinated, Hughie watched the ice travel toward her until the men pushed it inside through one of the loading spaces.

She knew the scaffolding would be raised higher as the ice was stacked, until it was near the roof. As each layer inside the house was completed, workers there spread marsh hay over it so that the slabs wouldn't be frozen together.

With a great sigh, Hughie turned away from watching the work. She must face up to meeting Cass. Since he wasn't out there on the ice, he would be inside waiting for her. As she walked toward the stable door, Hughie hoped Jerry was somewhere nearby, watching.

She could feel a trembling inside her that rose all the way to the skin of her face and her lips. She took a deep breath. Get it over with and get that locket back, Hughie, she told herself.

She opened the door and entered a small room that had harness parts and tools hanging on the walls. The dirt floor was covered with straw. A door straight ahead opened into the horse stalls beyond, and to the left was a door into an office. No one was in sight. She had just closed the door behind her when Cass appeared in the office doorway.

"Hello, honey," he said.

The first thing Hughie noticed was that Cass was

wearing a sweater over his flannel shirt and had taken off his coat. Where was the coat? She might be able to reach into the pocket, snatch out the chain and locket, and run.

"Well, cat got your tongue, missy? Come on in." Cass stood back from the doorway, motioning her to enter. She walked quickly past him. The sun shone through the weather-stained glass of a window on the south side, opposite the door, casting dust-filled light beams across the room.

Hughie looked about quickly. Yes, the coat was hanging on the wall to the left of the door. There was a desk under the dirty window, with an old dining room chair behind it. Along the east wall was an old leather-covered couch. Horsehair stuffing showed through breaks in the cracked leather.

Cass pulled the door closed behind him. Hughie was startled to see him turn a key in the lock. Leaving the key in place, he turned to face her as she stood in front of the desk, staring at him.

"Now, honey, you don't need to look so scared," he said. "Old Cass ain't gonna hurt you. Just set yourself down on the couch, and we'll talk a bit about what I found."

Without taking his invitation to sit down, Hughie asked, "Is it my gold locket and chain?"

Cass smiled broadly, showing his stained teeth, and stepped toward her. "That's what you were lookin' for, ain't it? Nice little picture of you inside it, too, so I knew it was yours. It's a real purty locket, and likely worth payin' the finder with somethin' nice—a reward, I think, is the word."

Hughie said, a note of hope in her voice, "Mr. Cass, I'll get some money for a reward if you'll give it back to me—maybe a dollar? She had never had that much money at one time in her life, but she had saved fifty-four cents and might be able to borrow the rest of it from Marty, who put every penny he got into his bank.

But Cass just laughed. "No, honey, it ain't money I want for a reward. I jest want you to be real nice to me while you're out here. The door's locked and ain't nobody gonna come in and bother us."

Hughie had an awful feeling of everything getting twisted together inside her as Cass stepped nearer and grasped the lapels of her coat.

"Sunshine makes it nice'n warm in here, honey. Let's take off your coat so's you kin be closer to me."

"No. I can't stay."

"It won't take long, but this coat is in the way. Come on, now, let's take it off."

"No. I'll keep it on."

Cass said, "Well, we'll at least unbutton it," and he did, pushing it back as he finished. Hughie stood still, knowing she'd need to give in a little to get her locket.

"There, that's better," he said, and ran his hands slowly down her body, inside the coat. Then he said, "You like that, honey? Let's start with a nice sweet kiss." He pulled her tight. Hughie could hardly breathe and turned her head, dodging his lips. Then she realized she had better let him kiss her and get it over with. She tried to relax her body.

"Show me my locket and then I'll kiss you," she said hopefully.

Cass felt some of the tension leave the girl. He

stroked her body again as he said, "First the kiss. And I've got something else I want to show you, too." His arms tightened around Hughie's waist. His face pressed against hers.

Hughie could make no sound at all, for her mouth and nose seemed buried in Cass's mustache. I can stand it just for a minute, she thought, to get my locket back. She made another conscious effort to relax.

Cass felt the change and held her even closer. Hughie thought the kiss would never end—that she'd suffocate first. But at last he pulled back an inch or two.

"That's better, little missy. I think you're ready for me to show you something else now." His voice was oily smooth and low.

He slid his arms slowly down her back, inside her coat, and pressed her close to him. "Mmmm—you're sweet, honey. I think it's time to show it to you."

"You mean my locket?" she gasped.

"Not yet." Cass scowled and pulled back a little, loosening his grip. His voice changed. "Now don't act so innocent. You know what I want to show you."

Hughie pushed against his chest as hard as she could with both hands, and Cass, losing his balance, fell back onto the couch. He shouted an oath.

"Jerry!" she yelled.

CHAPTER * 13

Not daring even to take time to reach into Cass's coat pocket, Hughie ran to the door and turned the key to unlock it. As she swung the door open, she saw Jerry running through the door to the stable. "I've got to get out of here!" she said and rushed outdoors, almost falling over Barney.

"Oh, Barney!" She dropped to her knees and hugged him.

Jerry followed her, pulling the door closed behind him. "Barney must have heard you yell in there, Hughie, because he broke loose to get to you."

Hughie kept a hand on Barney's collar as she got to her feet. "I—guess I didn't tie the rope very well." She looked up at Jerry. "Thanks for coming—"

"Hughie, you looked so scared when you came running out. What happened in there? Did you get the locket?"

They walked away from the building. Hughie didn't answer for a moment. Then the horror she had felt swept over her again, and she began to cry. All she could say was, "No."

Jerry was staring at her, not sure what had happened or what to say.

"Oh, hey, Hughie—we'll get it back. Don't cry."

Hughie could only sob. Jerry shifted uncomfortably

from foot to foot. He reached out and awkwardly patted her shoulder.

When the sobs finally stopped, he said, ''Aw, Hughie—it'll be all right. He's gotta give it back to you. Come on, let's tie Barney up and go out and watch the men for a little while.''

"I don't want anyone to see me." Hughie got the words out with great effort.

Jerry turned her around, toward the road. "All right. We'll walk this way until you feel better. Barney can go with us."

They walked slowly past the snow fort and out toward the road, Barney staying close at Hughie's side, even though she had let go of his collar. She was trying to stop crying, but they were in front of the house before she was able to talk. "It's—it's not just the locket, Jerry. He—he was going to—" she couldn't go on.

Jerry stared at her. "You mean that guy Cass tried to—"

Hughie nodded and began to cry again.

"That stinkin' dirty old man!" They had stopped walking, and Jerry turned to look at her. "You want me to go back in there and knock him down?"

Hughie took hold of his arm. "No, Jerry! You'll just get in trouble and lose your job."

"Well, he can't get away with that! And he didn't even give you back your locket."

Hughie knew she must look awful. She turned away, so that Jerry wouldn't see her looking so ugly, and tried to breathe deeply. She pulled her handkerchief from her coat pocket and wiped her eyes, her nose, and her mouth. There was a fleck of chewing tobacco on her handkerchief. She shuddered and took another deep breath.

"I think I'm all right now," she said and turned toward the lake. "Let's go back."

"Yeah. I want to see how much they got done since this morning."

They walked slowly, Barney following them. They were about fifty feet from the stable when Hughie tugged at Jerry's arm. "There he is," she said. "I don't want to catch up to him."

Cass had just come out the door. He was wearing his coat now, and he headed out toward the lake, not seeming to have noticed the two young people. They followed, keeping their distance behind him, and saw him go out onto the ice.

"I'll take Barney over and tie him up," Jerry said. At that same moment, Cass shouted an order to the men.

Barney growled and stood still for a moment, his thick fur around his neck standing out stiffly. Then, as Jerry reached for his collar, the dog plunged ahead, running full speed toward the ice.

"Barney, no!" Hughie called, but Barney paid no attention. Out onto the ice he ran. Jerry and Hughie ran too.

The big dog headed unhesitatingly toward Cass, who was now on the section of ice right next to the open area of dark water. As he had done before, Barney bit at Cass's boot. Cass tried to shake him off, swearing loudly. Barney's response was to go for Cass's trouser leg. With a mighty kick, Cass sent him sprawling, sliding toward the edge of the ice.

"Barney! Barney!" Hughie shouted. Horrified, she saw the dog slide off the edge and into the frigid lake,

Jerry wasted no time. As fast as he could, he ran out onto the ice and stopped close to where Barney was struggling. He stretched out flat on the ice, reaching for Barney's collar, and grabbed it just before the dog's head sank out of reach.

"Hold my legs, someone!" Jerry yelled. "I'm slipping!"

Lars Olson had dropped his ice chisel and was there to help. "Hold on, kid," he said. "Ve'll get him out!"

Two other workmen were beside him.

"Mike, hold Yerry's feet," Lars said to the smaller of the two, and Mike took a firm grip on Jerry's boots. "Now you, Bill, get on dat side! I tink ve pull the dog out!" Bill and Lars, flat on the ice, one on each side of Jerry, plunged their gloved hands into the frigid water. Each grasped one of the dog's front legs.

Barney was pawing frantically, and Jerry was having a hard time keeping his grip on the dog's collar. The men tried hard, but they couldn't lift the big dog from the water.

Mr. Owens came running from where he'd been directing the ice cutting. He reached out and grasped the handle of a long prod one of the men was holding, a tool with a hooked end for pulling ice blocks.

"Let's get this prod hooked under his collar, men," Mr. Owens said. In a moment, this was done. "Now, all pull!" he called. Lars, Bill, Jerry, and Mr. Owens struggled to lift the frightened dog from the water, and a moment later Barney stood on the ice with water streaming from him, shaking with fear and cold.

Hughie pushed her way into their midst. "Oh, Barney!" she cried and hugged the dripping dog. One of the men came running from the stable with a horse blanket and wrapped it around him.

Mr. Owens said, "Lars, you and Bill had better go in and get yourselves dry and warm, too."

Jerry was on his feet, pulling off his wet mittens. "I'll help you get him to the house, Hughie," he said. "We've got to dry him off as soon as we can."

Cass had been standing back from all the action. "I told you to keep that mutt away from me," he said. Should've let him drown before he bites someone else."

"That's enough, Cass," Mr. Owens said. "I'll talk to you later. Now let's get back on the job here."

Hughie and Jerry, with Barney between them, reached the back porch.

"Mama! We've got to bring Barney inside!" Hughie shouted. Nora and Beth ran over from where they'd been playing. They opened the door to the storeroom. Barney, with the four young people surrounding him, stood shaking with cold in spite of the horse blanket wrapped around him.

Mrs. Riley hurried out from the kitchen. She saw the dog with his thick fur a sodden mass. "Oh, Barney! What a day for a swim!"

"Cass kicked him into the water, Mrs. Riley," Jerry said.

"He'd have been caught under the ice and drowned if Jerry hadn't grabbed his collar and held him," Hughie said. "We gotta get him warmed up, Mama. He's shivering!"

"I see he is. For once, you can bring him into the kitchen. Put that horse blanket on the floor alongside the range—but mind you put it where Minnie and I won't be falling over the dog. And Hughie, there's a big old towel under the sink. Get it and rub Barney with it until he stops shaking."

A few minutes later, Barney was settled on the blanket, with Hughie, Nora, and Beth all helping to rub him dry.

Jerry stood back, watching. "I've got to go now, Hughie," he said. While they were all gathered in the warm kitchen, he had taken off his wet coat and his stocking cap. Now he picked up the coat and touched the cold, wet sleeves gingerly with hands still red from the icy water.

Mrs. Riley looked up from where she was rolling out pie crust. "Jerry, you can't work in that wet coat. Hughie, go out and get Papa's old jacket that's hanging out in the storeroom. We'll dry Jerry's coat here in the kitchen while he's working. Get him some dry mittens, too. And Jerry, warm your hands before you go out— hold them over the stove. And help yourself to some cookies."

Jerry grinned widely. "Yes, ma'am—to everything, especially the cookies!"

When Hughie came back into the kitchen with the dry jacket and mittens for Jerry, he was acting on Mrs. Riley's advice, with his mouth full of cookies as he warmed his hands.

"I'd better get out to the stable and go to work now," he said a few minutes later. Wearing the borrowed jacket, he put on his cap and the dry mittens. As he started for the door, he bent down to pat Barney's head. "You stay off the ice after this, Barney, old boy. You think you're through with this horse blanket now? Old Cass'll get mad if it isn't in the stable."

As if to answer, Barney stood up and Jerry pulled the blanket from under him. The dog's wagging tail drummed against Jerry's legs.

"He's saying 'Thank you for saving me, Jerry,' " Nora cried. But a moment later, her laughter changed to a shriek as Barney shook himself vigorously to get more wetness out of his thick fur coat.

Later in the afternoon Marty and Jim came in from sledding. Hughie was sitting at the kitchen table trying to do her homework.

"Rats!" she said as she added a long column of three- and four-digit numbers.

Jim said, "Rats! That's a fine thing to call your brothers."

Usually, this would have drawn a big grin and a smart answer from Hughie. But she just smiled a little and said, "Not you, this arithmetic problem."

"You sick or somethin', Hughie—doing' your homework already?" Jim asked. "We thought you were gonna come over to the hill and bobsled with us." He discovered Barney's presence. "And why's Barney in the house?"

Nora piped up. "Barney almost got drownded in the lake, and Jerry saved him."

"Huh? Barney knows better than to jump in the lake in winter."

Hughie said, "Cass kicked him again and shoved him

in. Jerry ran over and grabbed his collar just in time to keep him from going under the ice. He never would have got out if it hadn't been for Jerry.'

"Oh, gee—poor Barney!" Marty was down on his knees petting the big dog, who was enjoying this special treatment.

Soon afterward, Jerry came back to get his own coat and mittens. "Thank you, Mrs. Riley," he said as he turned to leave.

"We owe much more to you, Jerry. We'd all miss Barney terribly—and Hughie says you're the one who saved his life."

"It wasn't just me. I couldn't have got him out of the water without the men helping."

"Just the same, you're welcome here any time, isn't he, Barney?"

The dog, now thoroughly dry, was panting with the warmth of the kitchen. Mrs. Riley decided it was time to put him outside.

He's dry now and he's getting much too warm by the stove. Take him back out, Hughie, and tie him up well this time."

"Okay, Mama. Come on, Barney."

Hughie and Barney followed Jerry out to the storeroom. She'd been worrying all afternoon about what she should do to get her locket back, so she was pleased to have a chance to talk to Jerry alone. He was the only one who knew about the locket *and* about Cass. Maybe he'd have a good idea.

As she reached for her coat, she said, "Wait a minute, Jerry. I need to ask you something."

Holding Barney by the collar, she went down the

back steps. Jerry walked over and got the rope. "Here you are, Barney." He ran the rope end through the loop and tied a square knot. "There. He can't pull that knot out. What did you want to ask me, Hughie?"

Hughie stood facing him, with her hands in her coat pockets. "I want to know what you think I should do. I'm in a real mess now. Can't get my locket—can't stand even to look at that man again."

Jerry looked down at the snowy path and rubbed a place smooth with one booted foot. After a moment he looked up. "I know what I'd do if I were you," he said. His bright blue eyes looked directly into Hughie's.

"What?"

"I'd tell my father the whole story. He'd tell Mr. Owens, and that would be the last you'd see of that Cass guy—ever! Owens will fire him in a jiffy when he knows what kind of fellow he is!"

"But Cass'd prob'ly take my locket with him and sell it." Hughie spoke in a voice so low that Jerry could hardly hear her. "And Grandma would never forgive me for losing it."

"Come on now, Hughie! When you talk to your folks you've got to tell them you lost it! Then your pa could tell Owens, and he'd get the locket from Cass."

"But Mama'll be mad at me too. She told me not to wear it."

Jerry turned as if to go. "Sometimes we just have to face the music and 'fess up to doing something wrong, Hughie. Like I had to when I was tossing a ball in the house and broke my mother's expensive vase."

"This is worse, Jerry."

"Why?" He looked back at her. "That vase couldn't

be fixed and it was real old, too. You'll get your locket back, good as ever, prob'ly."

Hughie looked down at her feet. "It's not just the locket. Papa'll be mad at me 'cause I went to meet Cass."

"Hughie! You didn't know what he'd do!"

"I did, kinda. I just didn't know how scared I'd get."

Jerry looked over at the stable. "I gotta go, Hughie. The horses will be brought in any minute. Just do like I say, and you'll feel a lot better and get your locket back too. Tell your folks everything." He smiled at Hughie, whose eyes were tear-filled. "Promise?"

She managed a slight smile and nodded. "Okay, Jerry. Thanks."

" 'Atta girl!" And he was gone.

At least he said 'atta girl, not 'atta boy! Hughie thought, and almost smiled again.

When the Riley family finally sat down to supper that evening, Hughie had made up her mind. Jerry was right. She would get Mama and Papa alone and tell them the whole story. She pushed her fried potatoes and knockwurst about on her plate and ate only a few bites.

"What's the matter, honey?" Papa asked. "You usually finish your knockwurst and ask for more, and you've hardly touched it this evening. Do you feel all right?"

"I'm just not hungry tonight, Papa."

"She's thinking about how Barney almost got drownded this afternoon," Nora said. "Hughie was awful scared-looking when they brought him inside to get dry."

"Jerry said that Cass guy kicked him right over the edge," Jim contributed. "He's mean."

Mr. Riley frowned. "Wonder if Owens knows about this."

"Cass kicked Barney a couple of other times too," Marty added. "And he never jokes with us like the other men do."

Mr. and Mrs. Riley exchanged glances. "I think I *will* have a talk with Owens," Papa said.

As Hughie got up from the table, she gathered her courage to whisper in her father's ear, "Papa, I need to tell you something else about Cass."

Mr. Riley looked at his oldest child inquiringly, but he just nodded and said, "After a while, honey."

"Bath time!" Mrs. Riley announced a few minutes later. The tin tub was already warming near the stove. Hughie poured in a few buckets of hot water from the stove reservoir, mixed with cold from the cistern pump. The Saturday-night bath schedule went on from there as usual.

When all the other children had gone to bed, Hughie came back to the kitchen in her nightgown, warm robe, and slippers. She and her parents were alone. Papa sat in his usual place at the end of the table.

"Now then, Hughie. Come sit near me and tell me what is bothering you."

Hughie took a deep breath. "Mama, you'd better hear this too." Mrs. Riley picked up her mending basket and moved closer.

"It started the day Grandma had to leave to go home

to Aunt Effie. You told me not to wear my beautiful locket when I went out to play—" Hughie's voice broke a bit. She swallowed hard and went on. "But I did, Mama. And it fell off somewhere—out on the ice, I think. I'm sorry, Mama, awful sorry."

Mrs. Riley didn't even look up from her darning. She said softly, "I thought something like that had happened, Hughie, or you'd have worn it to church. You haven't found it?"

"No, but I know where it is. Mr. Cass has it. He said he found it, and Jerry saw him pick up something shiny the first day they worked out on the ice."

"Well, all we have to do is ask him for it then," Papa said. "He surely knows it must belong to someone in this family."

"He knows it's mine 'cause he opened it and saw the picture Grandma put in it," Hughie said. "But he won't give it back." She started to cry.

And then, little by little, the whole story of Cass coming to the cellar came out. Even harder to tell was that she had gone to meet him in the stable and why she got so scared and ran out.

"That was just before he kicked Barney. And that was my fault, too. I—I didn't tie the rope right. Oh, Papa, Mama, I feel so awful!"

But it was out at last. Papa was up and walking back and forth, trying to keep calm. Hughie had never heard him swear before, but she heard him now. Finally he turned to her.

"Hughie, don't you remember that your mother told you, before the men got here, that if Cass tried anything again you should come to me right away?"

Hughie was crying so hard she could scarcely speak. "Yes—Papa. I know I did wrong."

He said, "Stand up, honey. Let your papa hold you now. It's all right. Just remember, if anything like that happens again—ever—you come to me right away." He was stroking Hughie's shaking shoulders. "Calm down now, child. Your mama and I love you so much it hurts us to see you hurt. Papa will go in and talk to Mr. Owens, and we'll get this all straightened out. You won't ever have to see that man Cass again."

CHAPTER * 14

Hughie slept so well that it was daylight before she woke. She thought of all that had happened on Saturday, and how much better she felt, now that she had told her parents the whole story. Leaving Nora and Beth to sleep a little longer, she began to dress.

When she went to the dresser to get her clean clothes, she could hardly keep from squealing with delight. There was her beautiful locket, right on top! Mr. Owens must have made Cass give it to Papa. This was Sunday. She'd wear it to church. With shaking fingers, she fastened the chain around her neck.

Sunday was the only day the ice crew didn't have to work, but most of the men got up early anyway. Some of them were in the dining room already, having breakfast. As she dressed, Hughie could hear them talking.

She was about to leave the bedroom when she heard the sound of a chair being pushed back. She opened her door just enough to see Cass, dressed in a suit, walking toward the stairway door. Then Hughie heard one of the men say, "That Cass was gettin' on my nerves. I'm glad he got the gate. Good riddance. Never knew a meaner cuss'n him."

So Cass was leaving! Pretending she'd heard nothing, Hughie went through the dining room with only a quick "Good morning." She didn't want to be there when

Cass came back downstairs. Hughie was glad Mr. Owens was not at his place at the head of the table, either. It would be hard to face him too, knowing that Papa had told him about her problems with Cass.

In the kitchen, her father was shaving at the sink, and Mama was frying pancakes at the stove. Minnie was there as usual to help with the serving.

Papa's voice had that strained sound it got when he was holding his chin up to shave under it, but he said, "Mornin', Hughie. Did you find something on your dresser?"

Hughie smiled. "Yes, Papa. I guess some good fairy came into my room last night." She gave him a kiss on his cheek just above the soap lather.

Mr. Riley laughed. "It's surely fine to be called a good fairy when you're as old and ugly as I am. Isn't that right, Minnie?"

Minnie looked mystified. "I ain't seen no good fairies lately, so I can't rightly say."

Hughie went over to hug her mother. "I love you, Mama," she whispered. She held the locket out from around her neck. "Isn't it beautiful? Thank you, Papa."

"Looks like Christmas again 'round here," Minnie said. "That's sure a pretty locket, Hughie. Real gold, ain't it?"

"Yes, real gold and real old. Grampa Hughes gave it to my grandma before they were married. I'm only going to wear it for special days, like Sunday. I sure don't want to lose it!"

Mrs. Riley said, "That old catch on the chain comes open easily, honey. So be very careful."

"You don't have to worry, Mama. I've learned some big lessons."

With an apron over her dress, Hughie took over the job of turning the bacon in the big skillet. She suddenly realized how hungry she was.

About ten minutes later, when Minnie had taken the platters of pancakes and bacon into the dining room, she came back with the latest news. "That Mr. Cass just left for good. Drayman's out there to take him and his trunk to the depot to catch the mornin' train to Chicago, the men said. Don't know how come he's leavin' so soon, but I never did like to wait on that man. I ain't gonna shed no tears over seein' him go!"

Later in the morning after the church service, Mr. Riley stayed inside for a short meeting with other adults and the pastor, while the young people went outside.

Hughie left her sisters with Genevieve Byrnes and the other little girls and walked over to join the seventh- and eighth-graders. The two Schultz girls and their brother Bill were there, with Tim Tompkins and Jerry. Hughie left her coat open.

"Hughie, where'd you get the pretty locket? It's just beautiful!" said Mary Schultz. "Does it open?"

"Yes, it opens," Hughie said, and explained that it was a gift from Grandma Hughes. " 'Cause I'm her oldest granddaughter, and I'm named after her." Carefully, she opened the locket, revealing the heart-shaped picture of herself in the right side and the other empty frame. Looking up, she caught Jerry's eye. He was smiling his approval.

"I'd love to have a locket just like that," Mary said. "Wish my grandma had one for me."

"Let's see this wonderful locket," her sister said. Mary moved over, and Julie reached out to take hold of it.

"Be careful how you handle it. It's real old," Hughie said.

"Too bad you don't have a picture for the other side." Julie let go of the locket and turned away. "That's supposed to be for your sweetheart, but I don't suppose you'll ever have one."

Hughie snapped her locket shut and pulled her coat closer. She had to fight to keep tears back and turned away so that the others wouldn't see.

Bill Schultz said, "Boy, Julie, if you don't sound catty. Doesn't she, Jerry?"

"Yeah, she sure does." Jerry was frowning at Julie.

Julie said, "Well, everybody knows Hughie's a tomboy, and fellows don't like tomboys, do they, Jerry?"

"Cut it out, Julie," he said, and turned his back.

Tim had been looking uncomfortably from one to another and decided it was time for action. He scooped up some snow, now wet and packable from the sunshine.

"Who wants a face washing?" he yelled. "How about Julie?"

He reached toward her. Julie screeched and ducked away. Jerry and Bill each made a snowball and started after Tim. "Wash his face, Bill, and I'll put one down his neck!" yelled Jerry.

The scuffling was on. Tim, trying to escape, ran out toward the sleighs and horses, at the hitching rail. The younger boys, including Jim and Mart, scooped up snowballs and ran over to join the fun. Snowballs flew and voices grew louder. Tim ran to escape, but slipped and fell right in front of the Byrneses' horse.

The mare whinnied and reared back on her hind legs. Bill and Jerry dropped their snowballs. Bill reached Tim first and grabbed his legs to pull him back, but one of the mare's hoofs came down briefly on his left shoulder. She reared again, but by then Bill had pulled Tim to safety.

"Easy there, Dolly." Jerry took hold of the horse's bridle and stroked her neck to soothe her until she quieted.

Tim was still lying in the snow, more frightened than hurt, when Hughie and the Schultz girls reached him. "Are you all right?" Hughie asked.

"I'm okay," Tim answered as he sat up. "But I'm sure glad my coat is thick. My shoulder feels kind of funny."

"Does it hurt much?" Hughie asked.

"A little. But sitting in this wet snow isn't very comfortable." He got to his feet.

The horse was calm now, and Jerry let go of the bridle. "Here comes my father," he said. "Let him look at your shoulder, Tim."

The adults were coming out of the church. "Dad, Dolly stepped on Tim's shoulder!" Jerry called. "Maybe you'd better have a look at it." In a moment, the doctor opened the top two buttons of Tim's coat.

"Blood on your shirt," he said. "I'll need to see if just the skin is broken or if it went deeper."

The young folks, all serious now, saw the red blotches as the doctor pulled Tim's coat farther back.

"Ooh, blood!" Julie shuddered. "I can't stand to see blood."

"I hope you're not the only one around if I ever cut myself, Sis," Bill said.

"Bill, take him into the church while I get my bag from the sleigh," Dr. Byrnes said. "It's just a surface wound, but I want to be sure it's clean."

Mr. and Mrs. Schultz were ready to start for home. "Come on, girls," Mr. Schultz called. "Bill can follow later."

Jerry took hold of Hughie's arm. "I want to hear about last night," he said. "Did you tell your folks about Cass?"

"Yes, and Papa went in and told Mr. Owens. He sent for Cass, and I guess he told him to go get the locket. Then he fired him—that's what the men are saying, and Cass left on the morning train."

"Golly, Hughie, I'm sure glad."

Mr. Riley, gathering his children, called, "Hughie, let's go!"

Quickly, Jerry added, "Your locket is real pretty, Hughie, and—so are you." He turned away before she could recover from surprise. Gazing after him, she saw that the backs of his ears under his stocking cap were red. He blushes, too! she thought, and turned with a big smile to join her family.

The next three weeks were busy. But each afternoon, when Hughie got home from school and before she began her chores, she went with Jim and Mart to the edge of the lake to check the ice cutting.

The straight-edged pool of dark water grew larger

day by day. The scaffolding on the icehouse rose high above the ground, as layers and layers of ice slabs were shoved inside.

Most of the jobs for which horses were needed were finished, and all but two of the animals had been loaded into a railroad freight car to go back to the city. Before long the horses would be pulling wagons filled with ice through the streets, delivering 25- or 50-pound chunks to families for their iceboxes.

Jerry's boss was Lars Olson, now that Cass was gone, and Lars gave him plenty of work to do. Jerry's main job was building up a woodpile next to the steam engine large enough to keep the boilers hot until he returned the next day. He used a sled to haul the cut wood from the main woodpile. Some days, Mart and Jim helped him. It gave them an excuse to watch how the steam engine worked.

It took an amazing amount of wood each day to keep a fire hot enough for the water in the boiler to produce steam.

"Ya, Yerry," Lars told his young helper, "you gotta feed a steam engine even more'n a horse. It eats up wood so fast yet!"

By Thursday, the first day of February, thirty feet of ice was stacked in the icehouse, filling it almost to the top of the openings. At last the large square marked off when they started was only a huge dark pool, with new thin ice forming each day. There were not many men left for Mrs. Riley to feed, for most of them had gone back to Chicago. Minnie no longer stayed to wash the supper dishes but went home right after the men were served.

"Mama, you look so tired," Hughie said after Papa had asked the blessing at the family supper table that evening. Mrs. Riley had dark circles under her eyes, and she had grown thin.

"I *am* tired, honey. But our job is almost over." She looked around the family group. "All of you look a bit worn yourselves. You've helped me a lot. I do have a wonderful family."

Later, after baby Rose and Beth were in bed, Hughie and her mother were finishing the supper dishes while Mr. Riley played a game of Old Maid with the boys and Nora at one end of the big table. Mrs. Riley, washing the last of the plates, said to Hughie in a low voice, "And you've helped most of all, honey. I don't know how I would manage without you."

Hughie hugged her mother. " 'Cause I'm the oldest—"

They both laughed.

"I keep thinking about how I'm going to Chicago," Hughie said.

"Sh-hh, Hughie! That's our secret. Maybe I shouldn't have told you, but I thought you needed something to cheer you up—something to dream about. You'll have to pretend to be surprised when Grandma tells you."

"I will! I'm a real good pretender," Hughie said.

"Old Maid! Papa's the Old Maid!" Nora cried out. The card game was over, and the private talk ended.

That Saturday was Jerry's last day to work for the ice company. The icehouse was filled, the openings boarded up, and the scaffolding taken apart and stored. The steam engine was allowed to cool down, and there was no more need for firewood. The last horses had been taken to the big barn in Chicago. Jerry's final jobs were to give the stable a good cleaning and help Lars Olson store the tools and planes.

Jerry finished his work in the early afternoon and got his last paycheck from Mr. Owens. When he came outside he saw Hughie taking Barney down to the lakeshore and went to join her.

Jerry showed Hughie his paycheck. He had been paid ten cents for every hour he worked, and Mr. Owens had added a whole dollar as a bonus.

"Gee, you're rich, Jerry! You can take a girl lots of places with that!"

Jerry grinned. "Yeah, guess I can."

"Well, Valentine's Day isn't far away. Julie will be happy you can take her to the party."

"Julie? Uh-unh. She's no fun. I think I'll take someone else."

"Oh?" Hughie reached down and patted Barney's head, bending over so that she wouldn't have to look at Jerry. "Have you got a new girl?"

"Yeah, I think so. She's got a nice gold locket, and I'm giving her this picture to put in it if she'll go to the party with me." As he put his paycheck back into his wallet, he took out a small photograph of himself and offered it to Hughie. "Here. Do you want it?"

Hughie looked at him in surprise. He was blushing. "You mean me?" she asked, and felt that familiar rise of warmth to her face too.

"Yeah."

"Well, sure I want the picture."

"And how about the party? Wanna go with me?"

"You bet your boots I do!"

Jerry looked down at his old work boots, now encrusted with bits of the "stinky stuff" Julie had complained about. "You mean you'd take these smelly old things?"

They both were laughing now. "Yup—stinky stuff and all."

Jerry grinned. " 'Atta girl, Hughie! You're better'n a brother any old time!"